*She lifted her eyes in time to see Gideon's mouth curve into a devastating smile.*

His eyes were bluer than blue as he leaned forward. "How would you like to go to Manhattan?"

Emma almost spit out her tea. "In New York City?"

"Unless they moved the buildings someplace else, yes, in New York City."

"Oh, sure," she replied, realizing the question was rhetorical. Had to be rhetorical. "Right after I get back from Paris."

"I'm serious."

He was? She studied his expression. He was. "Why?"

"Why, what?"

"Why are you asking me to New York?" There had to be a catch. The request was too spectacular, too out of the blue. People didn't just hand out trips to New York City.

"Because I have to go, and I could use an assistant," he replied with a shrug.

And there it was. He needed a secretary. She should have realized earlier. Why else would he ask her?

Dear Reader,

I'm married to a sailing enthusiast. On our first date he took me to a maritime museum, and while, as a landlubber, I was only mildly entertained by the exhibits, I knew this sea-loving Prince Charming was the man for me. So when I started writing *The Cinderella Bride* it seemed only fitting that Emma O'Rourke's prince sailed into Boston Harbor to sweep her off her feet.

Of course, Emma doesn't recognize her prince. How can she, when she doesn't believe in fairy tales or happy endings? Then again, neither does Gideon Kent. Both of them are so convinced dreams don't come true they can't see what's standing right in front of them. Fortunately, love has a way of bringing out the dream in all of us. Gideon and Emma are about to find out that with the right person, fairy tales *can* come true.

Emma reminded me of so many women I know— hardworking, dedicated and practical minded to a fault. I loved giving her a happy ending. And Gideon—well, I fell in love with him the minute he stepped on the page. I hope you enjoy reading their journey toward each other as much as I enjoyed creating it.

Best wishes

Barbara Wallace

P.S. As I mentioned above, I am a hopeless landlubber, married to a sailor. I tried to get the nautical terms as correct as possible, but if I missed one I hope you'll understand.

# BARBARA WALLACE
## *The Cinderella Bride*

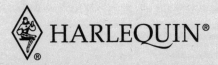

TORONTO • NEW YORK • LONDON
AMSTERDAM • PARIS • SYDNEY • HAMBURG
STOCKHOLM • ATHENS • TOKYO • MILAN • MADRID
PRAGUE • WARSAW • BUDAPEST • AUCKLAND

Recycling programs
for this product may
not exist in your area.

ISBN-13: 978-0-373-74069-7

THE CINDERELLA BRIDE

First North American Publication 2010

Copyright © 2010 by Barbara Wallace

**Printed in U.S.A.**

**Barbara Wallace** has been a lifelong romantic and daydreamer, so it's not surprising she decided to become a writer at age eight. However, it wasn't until a coworker handed her a romance novel that she knew where her stories belonged. For years she limited her dream to nights, weekends and commuter train trips, while working as a communications specialist, PR freelancer and full-time mom. At the urging of her family she finally chucked the day job and pursued writing full time—and couldn't be happier.

Barbara lives in Massachusetts with her husband, their teenage son and two very spoiled self-centered cats (as if there could be any other kind). Readers can visit her at www.barbarawallace.com, and find her on Facebook. She'd love to hear from you.

To Peter and Andrew,
who put up with a lot so I could chase my dream of
becoming a published author, and to Mom and Dad,
who always believed I could do it.

# CHAPTER ONE

NORMAL BOSSES DIDN'T MAKE their secretaries risk pneumonia hand-delivering financials. They let them stay in nice dry offices, typing on computers and answering the phone.

Unfortunately, Emma O'Rourke mused, she didn't have a normal boss. She worked for Mariah Kent, and when the matriarch of Kent Hotels said "jump," you didn't just jump, you asked how high, how far and if you should pack a parachute.

And so here she was, freezing on the docks of Boston Harbor.

*No matter what, do not leave that dock without Gideon's response.* Mrs. Kent's orders were beyond explicit. Emma sighed. Days like today she really, *really* hated her job.

Teeth clacking, she wrapped her blazer a little tighter, the thick manila envelope clutched against her chest crackling. She should have worn a coat. The navy-blue hotel uniform was designed to look crisp and efficient, not to withstand the elements. While downtown the skyscrapers created a sort of insulated bubble, here on the harbor the wind blew off the water, turning an already gray day raw. There was a mist in the air, too, moisture Emma swore hadn't appeared until she'd exited the parking garage.

Off in the distance, a boat zigzagged its way across the water, white sails billowing. Who sailed in New England in October, anyway? Apparently Mariah Kent's prodigal grandson. From the way he kept sailing parallel to the marina, he wasn't in a hurry to come home.

The mist turned to drizzle. Terrific. Now Emma's misery was complete. She freed a strand of copper hair from her damp cheek. By the time she got back to the Fairlane, she was going to look like a drowned rat.

"Hey!"

A brusque voice pulled her attention back to the water. Son of a gun, the boat was actually drifting toward the pier. A lone man knelt at the front, fussing beneath the front sail. He wore a baseball cap and nylon pants. As the boat drifted closer, he lifted his arm, and she saw a large split in the seam of his fisherman's sweater.

This was Gideon Kent, the prized grandson she'd stood freezing for?

*Thud!* A thick coil of rope landed on the dock. Emma jumped back to avoid it hitting her feet.

"Loop that over the piling."

Apparently he meant her. She looked around for a dry place to leave the envelope. There wasn't one, so she tucked the papers under her arm. The rope was coarse and wet, with a large loop at one end. Grimacing at the sogginess oozing around her fingers, she slipped the loop over a nearby post and stepped back.

"Not like that," he snapped. "Go up through the other eye splice, then over the piling."

*It mattered?*

"So the other boat can get out," he added, reading her thoughts.

*Oh, sure.* The owner of the other boat probably couldn't wait to sail on a day like today. She grabbed the rope again.

Naturally, Gideon's boat drifted with the current, dragging the line taut, and forcing her to pull with both hands in order to gain slack. Something that wasn't so easy to do with an envelope under your arm. Eventually, however, after much wrestling, she inched the soggy cable free. She had no clue what an eye splice was, but there was a gap where the other rope was tied to the pole. Water streamed onto her shoes as she folded the rope and threaded it through the space, as if threading a needle. Since no one bellowed a correction at her, she assumed she had guessed correctly.

"When you're done, you can head aft and do the same with the stern line," he said instead.

He was kidding right? He expected her to do this a second time? "Mr. Kent—"

"Boat's not going to secure itself."

"Boat's not going to secure itself," Emma muttered under her breath as she walked down the pier toward the second rope. Like the first, the thick nylon was waterlogged, leaving her hands wet and her legs splattered with seawater.

"The line secure?" he asked a couple seconds later.

If it wasn't, he could secure the darn thing himself. She stepped aside so he could see her handiwork.

"Good job," he stated. Despite her annoyance, the compliment gave her a rush of pride. "Now you can tell me what you're doing here."

Besides freezing to death? Unable to find a place to wipe her hands, Emma stuffed them into her pockets, discreetly drying them on her skirt lining. "I'm Emma O'Rourke, your grandmother's personal assistant," she said.

Gideon didn't respond, choosing instead to look her up and down assessingly. Her brief moment of pride faded, replaced by a familiar self-consciousness that washed over her from head to toe. Suppressing the urge to duck her head, she held out the rain-spotted envelope. "Mrs. Kent wanted me to deliver this."

Still no response. He stared for several more seconds, as if she'd just offered him a drowned rat, then turned away in dismissal.

Emma sniffed in surprise. Maybe he hadn't heard her, what with the wind and all. "Mr. Kent—"

"You can put the financials in the cabin."

Apparently he had heard her. He gave her another one of those assessing looks. "That's what's in the envelope, right? Financials for the last, what, two years?"

"Three."

"Like the extra year would tip the scale." He said the words so softly Emma doubted she was supposed to hear. When Mrs. Kent had first told her of Gideon's visit, she'd said her grandson was somewhat estranged from the family. "Just throw them on the desk," he said, with a resigned sigh that, again, she wondered if she were supposed to hear.

"I'm afraid it's not that simple," she replied.

"Why? Don't tell me you like standing around in the rain."

Oh, sure, didn't everyone? "There's a letter in the packet, and your grandmother expects a response."

"Mariah expects a lot of things." He wiped his hands on his thighs. "Doesn't mean you have to listen."

He was kidding, right? Everyone listened to Mariah Kent. Not listening to her would be like…

Like saying no to your grandmother.

"I only need five minutes," Emma insisted. "Then I'll be out of your hair."

"Appreciate the expediency, but that's five more minutes than I have at the moment.

According to the weather forecast, this rain's going to turn into a major storm front. I really do have to fasten down the boat."

*Yay,* Emma thought to herself. "Exactly how long does fastening down take?"

"As long as it takes." Stepping to the edge of the boat, he ducked his head under the lifeline and leaned close. "So I hope you like rain, Miss…"

Emma blinked. Up close his eyes went from merely scrutinizing to downright penetrating. A shade lighter than a sunny day, they had a blue brilliance that hit you long before you looked into them. Heat, the first warmth she'd felt since arriving at the marina, rippled through her.

He arched a brow, and she realized he was waiting for an acknowledgment. "O'Rourke. Emma O'Rourke. And I'll be fine."

"Fine?" Skepticism laced his voice.

"Don't have much choice, do I? Your grandmother expects me to return with an answer."

"Do you always do what Mariah wants?"

"It's my job."

"It's above and beyond," he replied, returning to the sails. "You must have a masochistic streak."

No, just a healthy distaste for unemployment.

Although at the moment, standing in line at the benefits office did hold a certain appeal. Emma shifted her weight from foot to foot, hoping motion might jump-start the circulation in her legs. What on earth had made her think she didn't need a coat?

"Do you want some help?" she called up to Gideon. "Two hands would make the job go faster."

He glanced at her over his shoulder. "Have you ever been on a boat?"

"Does the Charlestown ferry count?"

"No, it doesn't." He resumed his work. "And you wouldn't be helping. It would take me twice as long to explain what to do."

Unfortunately, he was probably right. She watched him wrap the sail around the boom with the arrogant grace of a man who'd completed the task hundreds of times. Every so often the wind would gust, causing the canvas to billow, and turning the waves around the pier choppy. But he maintained control, steadying himself on what she realized must be incredibly strong legs. A man in charge of his environment.

In spite of her annoyance, she was impressed.

"You know," he said, jarring her from her thoughts, "playing Little Match Girl won't make me go faster, either."

Emma gave him a confused look. "Playing who?"

"Little Match Girl. You know, the little girl trudging through the snowstorm looking for someone to buy some matches? It's a children's fable."

"I must have missed that one." She wasn't much into fairy tales. Wishing for Prince Charming was more her mother's style.

"She dies."

"What?" Emma looked up in surprise.

"The Little Match Girl. She dies. Freezes to death, actually."

Now that sounded more realistic. "Don't worry," Emma said, pretty sure he wasn't. "I'm not planning on dying."

"Uh-huh."

"Really, I'm fine." Of course, if he actually felt concern, he would give her five minutes.

They'd spent almost that long arguing about the match girl.

The drizzle grew heavier, hard enough to qualify as light rain now. Emma wiped the moisture from her face. Maybe she was carrying job dedication too far. Surely Mrs. Kent would understand if she opted against catching pneumonia while her grandson played stubborn little games.

*No matter what, do not leave that dock without Gideon's response.*

She sighed. Apparently Mrs. Kent knew her grandson all too well.

*Oh, for crying out loud...* Gideon tied the line off with a yank. Mariah had done this on purpose, sending some willowy, doe-eyed sentry to stand in the rain and make him feel guilty. And it had worked, dammit. Only a heartless ogre could concentrate with those brown eyes watching him.

"Why don't you go wait someplace warm?" he snapped. He wasn't giving her a choice, although she acted as if he was.

"I told you, I'm fine."

Right. That's why she was shivering.

No, not shivering. Bouncing. Rising up

and down on her toes and trying desperately to hide her discomfort. Rain beaded on her flimsy hotel uniform as well as on her hair, turning it to burnished copper.

*Dammit.* Dropping the rope, he channeled all his annoyance into one last sigh and stepped onto the dock. "Come on."

Little Miss Match Girl started; she'd been lost in thought.

"You said you needed five minutes," he said. "I'm giving you five minutes."

As she had with her misery before, she tried disguising her relief, and failed. "I thought you were fastening down the boat."

"I changed my mind. Now come on. And watch your step."

He took her by the elbow and propelled her aboard. The warmth of her skin surprised him. He would have guessed it would feel as cold as the weather.

"Where are we going?" she asked.

"To the cabin. You might not mind standing in the rain, but I prefer to conduct business inside where it's dry."

Her heels clattered as she dutifully accompanied him, her steps, he noted, matching his stride for stride. For a Little Match Girl, she wasn't all that little. In fact, she was close to his height. That made her, what—five foot ten or so without heels? Funny, when he first saw her, he'd thought she was smaller, more waiflike. He blamed those soft, brown eyes.

Warm air drifted up around them as he removed the hatch boards. He'd fired up the wood stove at sunrise and the trapped heat remained. Feeling it wash over him, Gideon realized exactly how cold he was after hours of exposure in the raw New England air. His body literally ached, he was so stiff and frozen. He could only imagine how Miss O'Rourke felt. Had she really intended to stand in the elements, waiting for him to finish? Because Mariah asked her to?

*"Ooomph!"*

Distracted by his thoughts, he hadn't noticed his visitor had stopped halfway down the companionway steps. His chest collided with her back, pitching her forward, and he had to grab her around the waist to keep her from falling. He might as well have grabbed a live ember from the stove. Heat rushed from her body to his. No longer cold or numb, he sucked in his breath, catching an intriguing whiff of vanilla as he did so.

He found himself speaking into her hair. "Something wrong, Miss O'Rourke?"

"I—um, no. It's just…this is lovely."

"It's even better once you're fully inside."

"Right. Sorry. For a second, I was… Never mind." She scampered down the last two steps and into the cabin. "Do you live here? On board?"

"When I can. My main house in Casco Bay."

"In Saint Martin. Your grandmother told me," she explained.

"Oh." What other details about his life had Mariah shared? Certainly not the biggest. That particular skeleton was buried way back in the Kent family closet.

Suddenly he was cold again, particularly his insides. Surprising how quickly the body heat dissipated once Miss O'Rourke moved away. "I need a cup of coffee. You want some?"

She looked at him as if he'd offered her the Holy Grail, but shook her head. "That's all right. I'm fine."

"Fine?"

"Uh-huh, fine."

*Fine.* It was the fifth time she'd said it, and he hated that word. As far as he was concerned, it the most irritating, dishonest word in the English language. Clearly, she was not fine. She was wet, windblown and hugging that wretched envelope as if it were insulation. And from the flash he'd caught in those brown eyes, she really, really wanted a cup of coffee.

For some reason, her refusal irritated him almost as much, if not more, than her Little Match Girl act.

Exhaling, he strode toward her, stopping only when the gap between them had closed to a few inches. "Last time I checked," he said, slowly pulling the envelope from her grip, "they didn't give out bonuses for sto-icism." He tossed the package on his desk. "So sit down, Miss O'Rourke, and have some coffee."

Emma didn't sit down. She stood frozen in place, listening to the sound of metal clank-ing against metal coming from the kitchen area. Though she hated to admit it, part of her was glad Gideon was forcing coffee on her. A strange combination of hot and cold, unlike anything she'd ever experienced, gripped her body. Her fingers and toes were number than numb, but her torso, at least the part where

Gideon's body had collided with hers, couldn't be warmer.

She hadn't meant to stop short on the stairs, but she'd been caught off guard. From Gideon's scruffy appearance, she'd expected some jumbled sailor's quarters filled with maps and equipment, not a haven of intimate elegance. With its cherry wood and wine-colored upholstery, the cabin was nicer than her own apartment. For a moment she'd been afraid to leave the steps lest she track water on the gleaming wood floor.

Fur brushed her leg, startling her into movement. Squatting, she came face-to-face with a large black cat. He looked at her with yellow eyes that rivaled Gideon's for intensity, and let out a hoarse meow.

"Well, hello there, you." She leaned down and scratched under the cat's chin. A sound resembling a small engine filled the cabin.

"You'll never get rid of him now." Gideon appeared bearing two steaming mugs. He thrust one in her direction. "Here, warm up while you talk. Do you want milk?"

The coffee did smell wonderful. Emma took the mug, pausing a moment to press it against her breastbone. The warmth spreading through her torso wasn't like the heat that had shot through her a few minutes before, but it was comforting nonetheless.

Meanwhile, her furry friend, annoyed that she'd removed her fingers from his fur, meowed and butted his head against her leg.

"Told you that you'd never get rid of him," Gideon said.

"I don't mind. He's very friendly."

"Easy to be friendly when you assume the whole world exists to do your bidding. Kind of like someone else we know," he added with a smirk. "Do you want milk?"

"No, black is fine."

Gideon gave her a look as he passed toward the galley.

"I thought sailors were superstitious," she called after him. "Aren't black cats supposed to bad luck?"

"Black cats, maybe," he called back, "but Hinckley doesn't believe he's a cat. More like an old man with fur." Gideon reappeared with a small bowl, which he set on the floor next to the steps. Hinckley raced over and began lapping with abandon, sending splatters of milk across the floor. That's when Emma noticed the space where his left hind leg should have been.

"An old man who's already had some bad luck," she observed.

"You mean the leg. A dog mauled him. By the time we crossed paths, the limb was too damaged to save, so the vet amputated."

"Doesn't seem to hold him back."

"Fortunately, the loss occurred when he was a kitten. It's harder when you're old enough to know what you've lost."

He added the last line in a lower voice, directed more to his coffee than to her. Emma almost thought they were talking about something other than the cat.

Silence filled the cabin as they sipped their coffee. Hinckley, having finished his milk, jumped up next to her and began to bath, using her thigh as a backstop. Smiling, she ran her fingertips through his fur. The cat responded by restarting his internal engine and laying his head on her lap.

"You like that, do you, sweetie?" Emma purred back.

The sound of Gideon clearing his throat brought the moment to an end. "You said you needed five minutes."

"Right." For a second there, she'd felt as at home as the cat, and acted that way. How embarrassing.

She looked around for the envelope, spotting it on Gideon's desk. Retrieving it would mean disturbing the cat. "Your grandmother enclosed a note with the financials, explaining everything."

"Why don't you give me the short version."

There wasn't exactly a long version. The note Mrs. Kent had enclosed was handwritten, and contained, at most, four lines. "She asks that you come to the office this afternoon. For a tea party."

His laugh was rich and throaty. "You're kidding, right? Mariah made you stand in the rain to tell me that?"

No, Mrs. Kent had asked her to hand-deliver the request. *He* had made her stand in the rain. "She wanted to be certain you received her invitation."

"You mean she wanted to make sure I didn't ignore it."

Was that a possibility? Given his earlier stubbornness, perhaps it was. Mrs. Kent's insistence that Emma stick around was making more and more sense. "She's simply happy you're back in Boston."

"She'd be the only one."

There it was again, the murmured tone that Emma wondered if she was supposed to hear.

"And what time is this little summit with crumpets?" he asked.

"Three o'clock."

"And not a moment before, right?" he said, smiling.

*He knew.* Emma couldn't help smiling back. Mrs. Kent made a lot of demands and requests, but she had one cardinal rule that trumped everything else: never interrupt her during *All My Loves.* Even her two sons, Jonathan and Andrew, knew the rule. Apparently, so did her grandson.

"Some things never change." For the first time since her arrival, she saw affection light up his eyes. "She still jotting off angry letters to the writers, too?"

"I've typed up five or six."

"She's easing up." Smile still in place, he raised his mug.

He took a long drink. Emma had never paid attention to the way a man drank before, but found herself unable to help watching Gideon. With the tension gone from his jaw, his mouth had a sensual quality to it. Soft and strong at the same time. And deliberate, she thought, noting the way his top lip slowly curled over the rim.

"So—" her own mouth had grown dry and she took a quick drink "—can I tell your grandmother you'll be there?"

Gideon finished his coffee, then set the mug on a nearby table. "I think it's been more than five minutes," he said, standing. "I have a deck to finish."

"What about tea?"

"You're welcome to stay and finish your coffee. Hinckley, I'm sure, would enjoy the company."

"What about—"

"Next time, I suggest you dress for the weather."

"Mr. Kent, please." He had one foot on the stair. Emma stood and caught his arm before he could take another step. She heard his sharp intake of breath as he turned around. Or maybe it was hers, as she reacted to the proximity of his stare. Was it her imagination or had his eyes changed shades, growing darker and more blue? "What should I tell your grandmother?"

That same stare traveled from her face to the hand on his arm. Slowly, he pulled away.

"Tell Mariah," he said, with a look that was enigmatic at best, "that she'll have to wait and see."

# CHAPTER TWO

IT TOOK LESS THAN A minute for Emma to follow Gideon topside. He felt her before he heard the click of her heels. Funny that, for someone he barely knew, she was quite predictable.

He was tossing fenders over the side to prevent the boat from smashing against the dock. When she passed him, he looked up. Their eyes locked, and he caught the full brunt of her perplexed annoyance. Clearly, she didn't appreciate his parting response. She had expected a concrete answer, and now no doubt thought he was being difficult for no reason.

She didn't realize that where Mariah was concerned, difficult was the name of the game. Especially when she wanted something. And she definitely wanted something. Case in point, sending the intriguing Miss O'Rourke instead of a courier service. Admiration stirred Gideon's blood as he watched the secretary's hips sway in cadence with her long legs. A courier service he could dismiss, but Miss O'Rourke… She was decidedly undismissable. A little too girl-next-door than he normally preferred, but impossible to ignore, nonetheless. He thought of her body pressed against his, and smiled, the memory chasing away the cold. Definitely impossible to ignore. And dollars to doughnuts, when she dried out, she'd be even more so. He stole another glance, and felt a new rush of heat. He could use a diversion on this visit. Unfortunately, Miss O'Rourke seemed like the kind of sweet young thing who expected long-term, and he didn't do long-term. If such a thing even existed. What number wife was Uncle Andrew on these days? Two? Three?

Then there were Gideon's parents, the poster children for false fronts. If Shakespeare were still alive, they'd inspire one heck of a farce.

No sir, long-term definitely didn't exist.

Why on earth was he thinking about relationships, anyway? Must be Boston, he decided, dropping another fender. Being back churned up thoughts he normally kept buried.

Fifteen minutes later, satisfied that the boat was secure, he returned to the cabin. Mariah's package lay on the desk where he'd left it. Three years of financials. What was his grandmother thinking?

"Does she think I'm going to see the numbers and suddenly return to the fold?" he asked Hinckley.

Well, the joke was on her. He followed the market. Kent Hotels might have stagnated a little over the last couple years, but they were basically healthy. The company didn't need him. Besides, it wasn't as if he belonged there, anyway.

*So why'd you come back?*

He'd asked himself that question all the way from Saint Martin, and the answer always came back to one thing: for Mariah. Had the request come from anyone else, he would have told them, in no uncertain terms, to leave him alone. But the request hadn't come from anyone else. And Mariah was the one Kent tie Gideon couldn't sever. Mariah, who had touched his cheek and told him his secret didn't matter. A lie, of course, but one that, at the time, was exactly what his distraught nineteen-year-old mind had needed to hear.

Hinckley yawned and rolled over. Gideon ran a hand across the cat's exposed belly, and the cabin filled with purring. Out of the corner of his eye, he saw the envelope. The stupid thing was mocking him. If he had any common sense at all, he'd ditch the package overboard, turn the boat around and sail back to Casco Bay before Mariah could rope him into whatever she had planned.

Instead, he opened the flap. Rows upon rows of figures greeted his eyes. Along with a single piece of Mariah's personal stationery. "Time to come home, Gideon," read the familiar script. "Tea is at three sharp. Don't be late."

*Time to come home.* Gideon tossed the package aside with a sigh. "Home" for him was an illusion that had died years ago. Around the same time he'd stopped believing in long-term and true love ever after.

*Achoo!*

Emma shoved her clipboard in front of her face, hoping to muffle the sneeze. From the look on Mariah Kent's face, it didn't work. The silver-haired woman peered regally over her half-glasses. "You're not getting sick, are you, Emma?"

"No, ma'am." Just cold. This morning's adventure on the waterfront hadn't quite left her bones yet. Fortunately, she'd been able to snag a spare uniform from the employee laundry. The dress was a size too small and rode up her legs every time she walked, but at least it was dry. That was more than she could say for her hair. Her still-damp ponytail hung down her back like the tail of a wet Irish setter.

Mrs. Kent didn't look sold on her answer. "Make sure you order yourself a cup of tea just in case," she said. "We don't want your sniffles turning into anything worse. Is your throat sore, too?"

"No, ma'am." Emma didn't have sniffles, either, but she knew better than to argue. Instead, she gathered her notes and rose to leave. It was almost two o'clock. "Will that be all?"

Mrs. Kent was already on her way to the chaise lounge in the corner of her suite. "I believe so. No, wait!" The older woman smiled. "Tell the kitchen to include extra meringue petit fours. Gideon will like those."

*If he shows up,* thought Emma as she

dutifully jotted down the request. His vague response had rubbed at her the whole way back from the waterfront. *Tell Mariah she'll have to wait and see.* Emma had stood out in the rain for that?

Mrs. Kent had taken his response in stride, chuckling about her grandson's stubbornness. "He always did hate being told what to do," she'd replied. "He'll be here, though. He's a good boy, and I can always count on him to do the right thing. Eventually."

The sound of voices brought Emma back to reality. She looked to the armoire and saw a beautiful blonde woman sobbing on the television.

"Oh, for crying out loud," Mrs. Kent muttered. "Are you still pining over that ex-husband? Make up your mind already."

Emma smiled as she headed to the door. The change from regal businesswoman to obsessed soap fan never ceased to amuse her. It was a side of the Kent matriarch most people didn't see, the softer, grandmotherly side, and it made it easier to endure some of the more outrageous demands of her job. Like this morning's debacle.

With Mrs. Kent sequestered for the next

hour, she had time to catch up on the work she'd missed this morning. Gideon had joked about her diligence, but Emma prided herself on being responsible. After all, someone had to be.

She placed a call to the chef confirming today's tea service, including the extra petit fours, then boiled a pot of water with the miniature coffeemaker she kept stashed behind her desk. Despite Mrs. Kent's insistence that she order coffee or tea from guest services, she felt more comfortable providing her own.

Fifteen minutes later she was inhaling the soothing aroma of orange pekoe. Mrs. Kent was right; tea did chase away the cold. Closing her eyes, Emma took a deep breath, then another, letting the warmth spread from her lungs to her body. Little by little the chill finally fled. She kicked off her pumps and flexed her nearly thawed toes. How on earth did people like Gideon stand being out in the elements for hours on end? In nothing but a ratty sweater, no less.

Maybe that explained the gruffness, she thought, taking a sip. His insides were frozen.

No, check that. She thought of their collision

on the stairs. He was anything but frozen. One brief contact had been enough to melt *her* insides. The memory made her shiver.

"Told you you'd catch a chill," a voice whispered in her ear.

"What the—" Emma started and dropped her cup. Tea sloshed everywhere. "Didn't your mother ever tell you not to sneak up on people?" she snapped.

The skin on the back of her hand stung where the tea had splashed. Shaking her fingers, she looked up into Gideon's blue eyes.

"On the contrary," he replied. "She preferred I make as little noise as possible." He nodded toward Emma's hand. "Did you burn yourself?"

"Nothing life threatening," she replied, regretting her outburst. "I'll be fine."

He made a sound resembling a strangled cough, and handed her a wad of tissues. "Here, dry yourself off."

"Thank—" The words died in her throat as his fingertips grazed the back of her hand, causing a flutter in the pit of her stomach. Startled again, she jerked away, letting the tissues float downward.

"Miss O'Rourke?"

"Yes?" His eyes had turned the most mesmerizing shade of sapphire. She couldn't stop staring at them. Not even when he nodded toward her desk.

"Your tea is pooling."

Emma blinked.

Her tea! Shaking off the trance, she saw a brown puddle spreading across her desk. Having ruined the correspondence she'd spent the last hour typing, it was making tracks toward the stack of manila files next to her phone.

"Oh no!" She grabbed another handful of tissues and threw them on the spill, hoping to stem the flow. The file contained original drawings for a renovation project at the Manhattan flagship hotel.

"Allow me." Gideon lifted the file so she could blot underneath. "Looks like your paperwork caught the brunt of the spill."

"Lucky me," she muttered, snatching more tissues. His chuckle would have annoyed her if she wasn't already battling embarrassment. She could feel Gideon watching her, the scrutiny flustering her so much that she nearly knocked over her remaining tea.

"You know," he said, moving the cup out

of her reach, "you were pretty lost in thought back there. Mind if I ask what had you so faraway?"

"Nothing important." Just him.

"Must have been somewhat important, because I knocked twice and you didn't hear me."

Emma's cheeks burned. She concentrated on throwing away lumps of wet tissues, hoping he wouldn't notice. "Your grandmother is waiting for you."

"I still have ten minutes. You know how she is about the daily cliff-hanger. Tell me, is anyone else attending this meeting?"

"Only you and Mrs. Kent as far as I know."

"Oh."

His voice had dropped a notch, sounding almost…disappointed? Emma abandoned her futile attempt to save the correspondence, and looked up. "Were you expecting someone else?"

"Not really." His answer had a note of forced nonchalance, then he changed the topic. "What's the damage?"

Substantial. The morning's mail was ruined, as was tomorrow's agenda notes and a half-dozen employee memos. Just thinking about how much time she would need to reprint them made Emma sigh aloud. "Fortunately, you saved the most important paperwork."

"You mean this?"

Opening the file, he started thumbing through the contents, his expression growing thoughtful. "We're renovating the Landmark?"

"So I've been told. Your uncle Andrew dropped off the designs this morning."

"Interesting. What do you think?"

"I only pass along the information," she replied. "I don't evaluate it."

"Is that diplomatic speak for 'I don't like it'?" He leaned forward, his eyes lit with what could only be described as mischief. "Come on, Miss O'Rourke, we both know you looked at the designs, if only to make sure the file was complete. What's your opinion?"

"I told you, I don't have one."

She reached for the folder, but he lifted it away. "Everyone has an opinion," he said. "Give me yours."

The truth? Gideon had guessed right; she hated the design. But she would never say so. The designer, Josh Silbermann, was considered the leader in contemporary design, and according to Andrew Kent, they were lucky to snag him. Since Andrew sat on more architectural and museum committees than she could count, she had to assume he knew what he was doing, and that she, in her inexperience, simply missed the point. "Your uncle is very excited about the plans."

Gideon looked unimpressed. "I'm sure he is. Andrew loves this sort of stuff. But you're avoiding my question. What is your opinion?"

"My opinion doesn't matter. I'm not the one making the decision."

He leaned forward. "Humor me."

"Why?"

"Because you're so determined to dodge the question, and that piques my curiosity. For example, what do you think of…" He fished through the file and pulled out a sketch, a stark study of gunmetal and black with splashes of ice blue. "What about this one?

She shook her head. *Figures*. He'd picked the ugliest sketch in the pile.

"Come on, Miss O'Rourke," Gideon urged, waving the sketch and grinning, "give it up."

Clearly, he wasn't going to stop until she said something. "Fine. It's cold."

"Cold?"

"The room. All that black and blue is far too harsh. I would prefer something warmer." *Like the blue of your eyes,* she caught herself thinking. "Plus the furniture looks uncomfortable."

"Really? Even these stainless steel padded benches?"

She caught the sarcasm. "I'm not sure even your cat would sleep on those."

"When I left, Hinckley was sleeping in the sink, so I wouldn't use him as a benchmark."

"I'm sure I'm simply missing the point."

"She says, desperately trying to regain her diplomacy," he replied with a chuckle. "Tell me, if you don't like this design, what *do* you like?"

Emma shrugged. Her experience in hotel rooms, particularly five-star hotel rooms, was limited to the Fairlane. "A comfortable bed."

"That's all? A good bed?"

"Okay, a *very* comfortable bed. What can I

say? I'm practical. After all, that's where I'd be spending the bulk of my time, right?"

He arched a brow. "You don't say."

"Sleeping," she stated hastily. Heat flooded every inch of her, and the mischievous glint in his eye didn't help. "If I'm staying in a hotel room, it's because I need a place to sleep."

"Of course." The glint persisted. Emma fought another rush of heat.

"But," Gideon continued, "if all you want is a bed, you can go to the local motel. You go to a hotel like the Landmark because you want atmosphere."

"The best for the best," she replied, parroting hotel management's catch phrase.

"More than that. You have to exceed their expectations." With the file still in his grip, he perched on the corner of her desk, close enough that Emma noticed his windburned knuckles. Outdoorsman's hands. Raw and weathered from work. The hands of a man who wasn't afraid to use them.

"…fantasies."

She jerked her attention back to Gideon's questioning stare.

"I was saying that for some people, a hotel room is their way of living out their fantasies," he said. "Which leads me back to my original question. What do you want in a hotel room?" He leaned a little closer. "Surely you have one or two fantasies of your own, Miss O'Rourke."

Beneath her ribs, Emma's heart skipped a beat. She could swear his eyes had grown two shades darker, as if he knew the path her mind had started to travel. It didn't help matters that his ear hovered close to her lips, as if he expected her to confess some little secret.

*He's talking about hotel marketing,* she reminded herself.

Yet the air between them had grown still. Disturbingly so. She hadn't realized before how Gideon's foot dangled perilously close to her calf. They hadn't made contact, but she could still feel him through her stockings.

She turned to her left, hoping to break the spell. "I doubt I could suggest anything marketing hasn't thought of already."

"Stop dodging the question."

"I'm not dodging." Not much, anyway. She grabbed the first stack of papers available and pretended to sort them. "I'm pretty basic when it comes to fantasies."

To her dismay, that earned her a melodic

chuckle. "Anyone ever tell you that you're too serious, Miss O'Rourke?"

Better serious than foolish. "Maybe I'm just easy to satisfy."

"Oh, I hope not. That would be a shame."

*Why?* Emma glanced over her shoulder at him. He was studying her again, with that probing look that made her skin come alive. "Three o'clock," she said, saved by the chiming of her desk clock. "Your grandmother's free now."

"Time then for my command appearance." He rose and put the sketches back in the file. "This has been a very interesting conversation, Miss O'Rourke. We'll have to do it again sometime."

"Sure," she answered. *Whenever you're killing time.*

She tried to ignore the way her stomach somersaulted at the suggestion.

Mariah Kent might weigh ninety pounds dripping wet, but it was ninety pounds of reinforced steel. When Gideon entered her suite, he found her seated regally at her desk, the same desk from which she'd run Kent Hotels for close to thirty-five years. How many afternoons had he spent sitting next to that desk, watching her work, listening to her advice?

*Treat every guest as if they're special, Gideon. Don't meet their expectations, exceed them.*

*Yes, Grandmother.*

That was a lifetime ago, he thought with a sigh. Back when he'd been a different person and believed Kent Hotels was his destiny.

"This is how you dress to see your grandmother?" Mariah asked, surveying his appearance with disdain. He'd come straight from the boat, and other than exchanging jeans for nylon pants, he still wore his sailing gear. "I distinctly remember telling you when you were growing up to always wear a tie."

"Sorry."

"No, you're not." She raised her cheek for a kiss, then patted his, the sparkle in her pale blue eyes betraying her affection. "You could have at least shaved. Is this how you dress for business in Saint Martin?"

"What can I say? Your summons was rather short notice."

"Not that short. Emma's been back for at least two hours."

"Yes, about that…" He sat in the chair across from Mariah's desk. "Was the personal summons really necessary?"

"I was afraid you might lose your way, after being gone for so long."

"Lose my way or change my mind?"

"With you, both are possibilities." Mariah smoothed the front of her designer suit, a silver that matched her hair. "Fortunately, I knew Emma would see to it you found your way."

As if on cue, his grandmother's assistant appeared, holding open the door for a waiter pushing an overladen tea service. Back in her office, she'd been blocked by her desk, but now he could appreciate how nicely the straight blue dress hugged her silhouette. Too bad she wore the matching blazer. He'd much prefer seeing her arms. Instead, he settled for studying the smooth curve of her calves. The desk had masked them, too.

"Are you ready for them to serve, Mrs. Kent?" she asked.

"Yes, thank you. Did you order yourself a

cup of tea like I suggested? You looked a little peaked."

"Yes, ma'am. I have a cup on my desk." Emma's eyes darted briefly in Gideon's direction, sparking the overwhelming urge to wink. If he did, he bet that pale skin would turn a very interesting shade of pink.

"Nice girl," Mariah said after Emma disappeared, leaving the floor butler to serve. "Takes her job seriously."

*A little too seriously,* thought Gideon. Then again, if their conversation had revealed anything, it was that Miss O'Rourke took a lot of things in life seriously. That didn't feel right, either, her practicality. What kind of woman didn't nurture a few romantic fantasies? The Caribbean was full of women her age champing at the bit for luxury and indulgence, and none of them, he wagered, would stand out in the rain because her job required it. If anyone should want pampering, it should be someone like Emma. But she didn't. She only wanted a comfortable bed.

He frowned. That wasn't right. Emma's lack of expectations were more suited to someone like him, someone with reason to be weary and cynical. Not a fresh-faced girl with freckles dotting her nose.

"Sugar?"

His grandmother's voice jerked him back to the present. From the other side of her desk, she eyed him with curiosity. "Do you still take three sugars?"

"No," he replied.

"Good. Too much sugar is bad for you, anyway," she said. "I'm glad you gave it up."

"I've given up a lot of things over the past ten years," he replied.

"Does that include your family?"

*What family?* "I've stayed in touch."

"E-mails," Mariah said with a frown. "Christmas cards. Phone calls on birthdays. That's not keeping in touch."

"I've been busy."

"No, you've been avoiding us, and it's high time you stopped." She set her teacup on its saucer with a resounding clink. "You need to come home."

*As if coming home was even possible.* Forcing a lightness in his voice, Gideon replied, "Aren't I already here?"

"I mean for good." Mariah looked him

square in the eye, her gaze reflecting every ounce of her mettle. "You're the eldest Kent grandchild. It's time you embraced your birthright."

Once upon a time those words would have meant everything to him. Now they simply lodged in his chest like an undigested meal. "Except for one thing," he replied.

Gideon leaned forward, dropping his voice to a conspiratorial murmur as he said what she seemed so intent on forgetting. "I'm not the eldest Kent grandchild."

Mariah didn't blink. She'd been expecting the comment, after all. "Your last name is Kent. And I need your help. Those are the only two things that matter."

*Surely you have one or two fantasies of your own.*

Try as she might, Emma couldn't dislodge Gideon's comment from her head. Two hours after their conversation, his words continued to repeat themselves in cadence with the pages spitting out of the printer. *Fantasies, fantasies, fantasies.*

*Just a comfortable bed.*

What was so wrong with her answer?

"Excuse me for being practical," she snapped at the printer. Dwelling on things out of her reach was a waste of time. She'd already spent too much of her life dealing with her mother's fantasy fallout. Emma didn't need disappointment of her own.

Which reminded her, she should call her mom and see if she found any leads at the unemployment office.

The printer made a loud clicking sound, drawing Emma's attention. Coming back to the present, she saw a red light blinking on the front panel.

"Don't tell me, I'm out of ink," she muttered. *Great.* At this rate she'd be forty before she got her desk cleared off.

*That's what you get for thinking about fantasies.*

Just then the door to Mrs. Kent's suite flew open. Gideon stared at her, his expression a study in tension. "Come on," he said, shutting the door. "I need a drink."

# CHAPTER THREE

BEFORE EMMA KNEW what was happening, he caught her elbow and pulled her toward the office door. "Do you know if the King Room serves a decent whiskey?"

"I, uh…" She was still trying to figure out why she was being dragged along.

"Never mind. They serve alcohol. We'll be fine."

"We?"

Gideon gave her a look. "You don't think I plan to drink alone, do you?"

So, what—he planned to drink with her? Nice of him to ask first. "I'm working."

"It's after five, Miss O'Rourke. Workday's over."

"For you, maybe, but I've got a pile of correspondence on my desk that your grandmother expects to go out in today's mail." Correspondence he'd helped delay.

"And the world must do what Mariah Kent expects, right?"

Emma started to say something about entitlement running in the family, but noted the tension in his jaw and thought better. Something had happened while Gideon was sequestered with grandmother. He was paler, and his eyes, sharp and probing a couple hours earlier, had dulled. In fact, his whole demeanor had a weariness that hadn't existed before.

The transformation jarred her, to say the least. Watching him impatiently pressing the elevator button, she had the overwhelming urge to reach out and squeeze his hand.

Which was why, when the elevator doors opened, she stepped in.

Designed to resemble a gentlemen's club, the King Room was the Fairlane's jewel, a private hideaway where guests could relax in oak-paneled splendor. When she walked through the frosted-glass doors, Emma could have sworn every head in the room turned her way. She could feel the unwelcoming gazes. This was a haven for guests, not hotel employees. Self-consciousness in overdrive, she tugged on her dress, hoping the dim lighting concealed its snugness.

Gideon, on the other hand, crossed the room with the nonchalance of a man who belonged, despite the fact that his sweater and jeans violated the bar's dress code. Emma couldn't help but marvel at his ease. No one rushed forward to politely offer one of the hotel's spare jackets, either, she noticed. Perhaps his last name bought him acceptance, but somehow she suspected the circumstances would be the same anywhere, family-owned establishment or not.

No sooner had they taken their seats than a waitress with a black ponytail and a perfectly fitting uniform approached. She flashed Emma a skeptical look before turning her attention and smile on Gideon. "Good evening. Will you be having cocktails or dinner?"

"Bruichladdich, straight up," Gideon clipped.

Although the name meant nothing to Emma, it must have registered with the waitress, for her eyes lit up with an intrigued gleam. "Certainly, sir." Her voice grew a notch smokier, as well. "It might take a moment, however. Our manager will have to retrieve a bottle from our reserve."

Gideon shrugged. "Fine. Miss O'Rourke, join me?"

"I'll have tea," she replied. "With milk."

The waitress nodded without looking in her direction. Emma wondered if the woman had heard her.

"Tea, Miss O'Rourke?" Gideon shot her a disappointed look. "You're missing out on a seriously good whiskey."

No doubt, judging from the way he'd impressed the waitress. "I'm sure that's true, but I'm also still on the clock."

"Ah, yes, Mariah's correspondence. Tell me," he asked, once the waitress had departed, "do you always do everything Mariah asks?"

That was a silly question. "Of course I do. It's my job."

"That doesn't mean you have to jump when she says jump."

Then he didn't know what working for his grandmother entailed. "What am I supposed to, slack off?"

"Would you even be able to?"

"If you're asking do I take my job seriously, the answer's yes."

"Really? I never would have guessed."

His sarcastic tone rankled Emma. No matter how poorly his reunion with his grandmother had gone, he didn't have to take out his frustration by mocking her. "What can I say?" she snapped. "Not everyone is lucky enough to be born a Kent."

She regretted the comment the second she'd said it. Not only was it beyond impertinent, it caused a shadow to break over Gideon's features, turning them dark and increasing their marked weariness. "Oh yeah." His voice was low and dull. "It's a real stroke of luck."

He lapsed into silence after that, his long fingers drawing patterns on the inlaid table. Emma stared at his wind-burned knuckles, wishing she'd bitten her tongue.

"I'm sorry," she said. "I had no right." When he didn't answer, she pushed herself away from the table. "Maybe I should just go and let—"

"Don't." Gideon reached out and caught her wrist. Barely a grip, but enough to stop her in her tracks.

"I thought maybe you'd like to be alone with your thoughts," she told him.

"If I wanted to be alone, I wouldn't have dragged you down here."

"But—"

"Sit down, Miss O'Rourke.

Slowly, she met his eyes. The blue had turned smoky, almost indigo in color. A new silence surrounded their table, heavier and more self-conscious than the one before. She looked down to where Gideon's fingers still encircled her wrist.

"Here you go." The waitress's voice broke the spell. She shot Emma an enigmatic look before placing a crystal tumbler in front of Gideon. "Sorry to keep you waiting, Mr. Kent."

Emma noticed that in addition to learning Gideon's identity, the waitress had undone two more buttons on her uniform. And was leaning forward more than usual. "If you need anything else, my name is Maddie. I'll be more than happy to accommodate you."

*I'll bet.* Emma tried not to roll her eyes. Talk about laying it on thick. Was Gideon impressed? "Do you have any artificial sweetener?" she asked.

Clearly annoyed at having to pull her attention away from him, the waitress shot her a glance. "We keep everything on the table," she replied in a sickeningly sweet voice. Emma knew that; she was just curious to see what Maddie would do.

The waitress didn't disappoint. "Here, let me get it for you," she said, leaning over far more than necessary to reach across the table. As she did, she angled her body so that Gideon got a good view of her perfectly formed cleavage.

"Thanks," Emma replied, her bravado shrinking. She'd caught a glimpse herself when Maddie had bent over. If there were a real competition, Emma wouldn't stand a chance, and they both knew it.

She waited until Maddie walked—or rather, strutted—to her next table, then pushed the container back into place. "I guess word of your arrival has trickled down the grapevine. Hope you weren't trying to remain incognito."

"Hmm." Gideon was busy studying the contents of his tumbler. He hadn't spoken since asking Emma to stay. She rubbed her wrist, surprised how her skin still tingled. Her reaction to his touch unnerved her, but not nearly as much as his silence did. His withdrawal made her insides ache.

"Mr. Kent?" He looked up from the amber liquid. "Is there anything I can do for you?"

Her question earned her a very strange smile. "Trying to compete with our waitress, Miss O'Rourke?"

"Hardly. You just look…" she shrugged "…out of sorts."

"And you, diligent employee that you are, want to help."

"A simple 'I'm fine' would suffice."

"I hate that word." He smiled again. This time a sparkle appeared with it, one that swept away any annoyance. "How long have you worked for Mariah, Miss O'Rourke?"

Emma added milk to her tea. "A little over a year."

"Most of her assistants don't last that long."

"So I've heard."

"Must be all that diligence."

"I like your grandmother."

"Even when you're standing in the rain?"

Emma laughed. "Even then. As you said,

she has a way of making people do what she wants."

"Don't I know it." Just like that, the sparkle dimmed from his eyes. Lifting his glass, he drained the whiskey in one long sip.

"Tell me something, Miss O'Rourke," he continued, studying his empty glass as he spoke. "Did you really dislike the Silbermann designs?"

"I didn't say I disliked them, per se."

"Miss O'Rourke…"

"I think your uncle Andrew is far more qualified to offer an opinion than I am."

"Besides, all you're interested in is a comfortable bed."

"Exactly."

Gideon nodded, and went back to studying his tumbler. Emma sipped her tea and tried not to squirm. Why did she feel like she'd given a wrong answer?

*Surely you have one or two fantasies….*

"Maybe we should put that theory to the test," she heard a voice say.

She lifted her eyes in time to see Gideon's mouth curve into a devastating smile. Awareness washed through her, pooling in one deep, very inappropriate spot. "W-what?"

Those eyes were bluer than blue as he leaned forward. The pool got a little deeper. "How would you like to go to Manhattan?"

Emma almost spat out her tea. "You mean, New York City?"

"Unless they move the buildings someplace else, yes, New York City."

"Oh, sure," she replied, realizing the question was rhetorical. Had to be rhetorical. "Right after I get back from Paris."

"I'm serious."

He was? She studied his expression. He was. "Why?"

"Why what?"

"Why are you asking me to go to New York?" There had to be a catch. The request was too spectacular, too out of the blue. People didn't just hand out trips to the Big Apple.

"Because I have to go, and I could use an assistant," he replied with a shrug.

And there it was. He needed a secretary. Emma should have realized that. Why else would he ask her?

"Does your grandmother know you're poaching her employees?" she asked.

"No, but I don't think she'll mind. The trip was her idea."

Emma sat back. "Really?"

"Unfortunately, yes. She wants me to meet with Ross Chamberlain."

Emma recognized the name from various memos and correspondence. He was Kent Hotels' largest nonfamily shareholder. "Why you—?" Her hand flew to her lips as she realized how insulting the question must sound. "Sorry. I only meant why isn't she sending one of the other Mr. Kents?" Why summon Gideon back to Boston, then send him to New York? That seemed a trifle eccentric, even for Mariah Kent.

"That, Miss O'Rourke, is the sixty-four thousand dollar question. Let's just say Mariah expects me to go."

And the world always did what she expected. Suddenly his earlier mood made sense.

But still, why take Emma along? Kent Hotels had a host of secretaries at his disposal. Both here and in New York.

"I don't want one of the secretaries in New York," he replied when she asked. "I want you."

She tried not to feel flattered by his answer. "What about your grandmother?"

"Believe me, Mariah will survive." He

grinned. "I mean, it's not like I'm taking away *All My Loves.*"

"Now that would be a real loss," Emma replied with a laugh.

"Then it's agreed. We'll leave tomorrow afternoon."

Emma's chuckle faded. "Tomorrow afternoon?"

"Is that a problem?"

"No, I suppose not. I just didn't realize you wanted to go so soon."

"The sooner I run this little 'errand,' the sooner I can get back to my own life. Can you arrange for the jet?"

"Certainly." Her head was swimming. She was flying to Manhattan. Tomorrow. That sort of thing didn't happen. Not in her world. A thrill tripped down her spine. "I'll go make the arrangements right now."

With that, she pushed herself away from the table. "Good night, Mr. Kent. Thank you for the tea."

"You're welcome. Don't work too hard. Oh, and Miss O'Rourke?" She was almost clear of the table when he called out to her.

"Yes, Mr. Kent?"

"We'll be staying at the Landmark." The

corner of his mouth slowly quirked in a teasing smile that curled Emma's toes. "I'm looking forward to hearing how you like the bed."

"Manhattan?" Leaning against the counter, Janet O'Rourke tapped her cigarette against the ashtray she held in her freshly manicured hand. "Don't they have secretaries in New York? Why'd he ask you?"

Emma shrugged. "He said he didn't want a secretary from New York. He's going on a business trip for his grandmother. Maybe he feels more comfortable taking someone from her office. And since I'm the only one he knows…" She shrugged again. Since Gideon issued his invitation, she'd asked herself the same question multiple times, and that was the best answer she could come up with.

"Or maybe—" her mother's eyes widened "—he's interested in more than business."

"You've been watching too many movies, Mom."

Leave it to her mother to raise that theory. Janet O'Rourke saw romance everywhere. That was one of her biggest problems.

"You never know. Is he good-looking?"

"Attractive," Emma admitted. And yes, she did know. She knew because of all the times she spent alone, fending for herself because Janet found true love—again—only to have to nurse her through a broken heart days later.

Emma's shoulders suddenly felt heavy. "How'd job hunting go?" she asked, changing the subject. "Any good leads?"

"Nothing that piqued my interest."

Not a surprise. Most work failed to interest her mother. "Well, maybe tomorrow."

"Actually..."

Emma stiffened. Whenever her mother started a sentence with the word *actually,* what followed wasn't good.

"Mary O'Leary and I were thinking of heading to the casino tomorrow. With luck, I'll hit big on the slots and won't have to worry about work."

"Wouldn't that be nice." Another one of Janet's pipe dreams. Her mother had dozens of them, every one leading to disappointment.

And Gideon Kent wondered why Emma didn't want more than a comfortable bed. As far as she could tell, wanting more only cost you in the long run. You were better off not wanting at all.

Life was safer that way.

# CHAPTER FOUR

"YOU EXPECT ME TO WHAT?"

Gideon couldn't decide which entertained him more: Hinckley making himself at home on the chaise lounge or the look on Mariah's face when he told her she would be cat-sitting. "I can't very well leave him locked on the boat while I'm gone. Someone has to feed him."

"That's what staff are for."

He didn't have the heart to tell her that in Hinckley's book, she *was* staff. Out of the corner of his eye he caught Emma's discreet smile, and resisted the urge to flash a conspiratorial wink.

Mariah's secretary was looking particularly blue today. Blue skirt, blue blazer, light blue turtleneck. Too bad this outfit wasn't as form-fitting as yesterday's dress. He liked seeing the curves.

"It's only for a couple days," he told his

grandmother. "You won't even know he's here." *Not much, anyway,* he added silently as he watched Hinckley flop on his side. His length took up more than half the seat. "You're the one who asked me to go to New York."

"I didn't realize my request would result in wild animals being left on my doorstep. Bad enough you've stolen my secretary. By the way, Emma, do you have the latest earnings per share projections?"

"Yes, ma'am. Jonathan Kent dropped them off this morning."

Hearing his father's name, Gideon felt a dullness akin to an ache form in his chest. Since his return to Boston, he'd noticed the man who'd raised him had been conspicuously absent. Gideon couldn't really blame him. No one liked being reminded of his mistakes. Or his wife's. If he were in Jonathan's shoes, Gideon would stay away, too.

He swallowed back his emotions. "I'd like a copy of that report."

"Already done, Mr. Kent."

"I should have known. Now you know why I stole her," he said to Mariah. "Who could resist such efficiency?"

"Hmm. And making me suffer for sending you on this trip had nothing to do with it," his grandmother replied.

"Don't be silly. That's Hinckley's job. Miss O'Rourke sealed her own fate."

She stared at him, her eyes impossibly large and dark. "Excuse me, I what?"

"With your efficiency," he replied. "How could I possibly take another assistant? Especially on such an important trip."

Actually, he didn't really know why he had asked her along. He didn't need a secretary for this meeting. Hell, he didn't have to stay overnight. He could wrap up his business with Chamberlain in a few hours. Maybe he did want to punish Mariah.

It was that conversation they'd had about the Landmark, that's what it was. The whole exchange had started as harmless flirting, a diversion while waiting for Mariah's show to end. But then Emma refused to offer her opinion. For crying out loud, his secretary in Saint Martin shared her opinions on everything, from the state of office supplies to Hinckley's habit of leaving 'dead mice' on the office doorstep. Ninety-nine percent of the time, Gideon didn't even have to ask.

But he practically had to drag the answer out of Emma. Why? Especially when her opinion made sense. The design *was* cold.

And who on earth wanted nothing but a comfortable bed? That particular comment had gnawed at him all night long. Emma's pragmatism bothered him. A woman like her, fresh and sweet…shouldn't she be full of silly romantic notions like sunken tubs built for two and balconies looking out at the stars?

She definitely should want more than a good night's sleep, he thought, eyeing her blue-clad figure.

"As long as you keep Gerard Ambiteau in his place, you can take every secretary we have in the building," Mariah was saying. She pressed her fingers to the bridge of her nose. "That man has no scruples whatsoever. I can feel him out there. He's waited years to find our weak spot, and now he's just waiting till the timing is right to make his move."

You couldn't miss the stress in her voice. Though he'd grown up listening to rants about Gerard Ambiteau, this was the most worked up Gideon had ever seen his grandmother. She was worried—genuinely worried. She also had a point. Right now, Ross Chamberlain was a weak spot that Ambiteau could easily take advantage of.

"I'll talk sense into Ross, don't you worry," he assured her.

She smiled "I know you will, darling. It's one of the reasons I asked you back home."

One of. He knew the other. The plan wasn't going to work.

Emma cleared her throat. "If you want to avoid rush hour traffic, we should consider leaving soon. I've already called the front desk. The car's ready whenever you are."

"See?" he said to Mariah. "Irresistibly efficient."

"I know. That's why I hired her."

"And why I poached her." He leaned over to kiss his grandmother's cheek, then stepped over to scratch the top of Hinckley's head. The cat was already sound asleep. "Behave," he said.

"Are you talking to me or the creature?"

"I'll let you two fight it out. Be careful, though. Hinckley fights dirty."

"So do I," Mariah replied.

Emma had retrieved her overnight bag and was already at the elevator when he finished his goodbyes. He caught up with her just as the doors slid open. "Are you ready to take a bite out of the Big Apple, Miss O'Rourke?"

"Ready as I'll ever be," she replied with a nervous smile.

She looked uneasy. Had done so, he realized, since he'd walked into Mariah's office. What was shyness yesterday was now far more pronounced, almost anxiety. He could see the tension in her ramrod posture as she stood beside him, watching the numbers count down. Guilt pricked his conscience.

"Everything all right?"

He watched her shoulders stiffen. "I'm fine," she replied shortly.

"Are you sure?" There were smudges under her eyes, dark hollows a shade lighter than her uniform. "You look tired."

"Really, I'm fine."

Then why was she chewing the inside of her cheek? It was the Little Match Girl act all over again, he thought with irritation. Why didn't she just say what was wrong instead of playing martyr?

Unless… A thought struck him. "Miss O'Rourke," he stated, "you're not anxious about being in New York with me, are you?"

She whipped her head around, her eyes a little wider than usual. "Of course not."

"Because I realize this trip is a little unorthodox."

"And I realize you wouldn't be anything but professional, no matter what— Never mind." She shook her head, leaving him to guess what she'd been about to say. "I'm fine, I promise."

He *hated* that word. There was no way on earth he was going to listen to her say it every five minutes on this trip.

The elevator doors parted and Emma started toward the lobby. "One minute, Miss O'Rourke." He stepped in front of her, blocking her progress. "Before we leave, we need to set a few ground rules."

"Ground rules?" Her features furrowed in confusion. "Like what?"

"First of all, I don't believe in mindless autonomy. I prefer my associates speak their minds. I expect *you* to speak your mind. Understand?"

She nodded.

"Good. Which leads me to ground rule number two. The next time you say the word *fine,* I'm going to hang you by that copper-colored ponytail of yours."

"What?" Her eyes grew dark and large, giving him a firsthand view of how expressive they could be. Expressive and innocent. Like the rest of her face. His own eyes fell to her lips, parted ever so slightly in surprise, and for a second he forgot what they were talking about.

She reminded him, however. "You don't want me saying the word *fine?*"

"No, I don't. Like I said, I prefer honest answers."

"'Fine' isn't honest?"

"My dear Miss O'Rourke." He caught her chin, forcing her gaze to meet his, so there would be no misunderstanding what he was about to say. "*Fine* is the most dishonest answer there is."

He released her, surprised at how reluctant his fingers were to break contact. "Now," he continued, stuffing his hand in his pocket, "let's start over. You look a little off this afternoon, Miss O'Rourke. Is everything all right?"

"Everything's *fi*—" She caught herself. "I was up late working. This trip came on short notice, so I had to put in extra hours to make sure my desk was cleared." Her concluding scowl was worthy of the most sulky of teenagers.

"Now, that's more like it." Gideon felt a chuckle rising in his throat. Her eyes were sparkling now, like two big, annoyed diamonds. He liked the look. Slipping the overnight bad from her grasp, he swung it over his shoulder, cutting off her impending protest. "Come along. We have a plane to catch."

What kind of person banned another person from using a word? Especially a perfectly useful word like *fine?* Emma wondered, annoyed. She chewed the inside of her cheek as she allowed Gideon to guide her through the private terminal at Logan Airport. Bad enough her racing thoughts had kept her up half the night. Now she had to make her tired brain think of synonyms? She was having enough trouble acting as if she knew how to navigate her way through an airport.

The terrible truth was that she wasn't fine. She was uptight, exhausted and nervous as could be. Though not, as Gideon suggested, about going to New York with him. No, she was nervous about getting there. Although she'd arranged dozens flights on the Kent corporate jet, she'd never actually seen the plane up close—she'd never seen a plane up close, period—and she was desperately trying to fake a practiced air.

Then there was Gideon, who overnight had morphed into a completely different person. Yesterday's sailor, while rugged and compelling, still had an element of accessibility to him. Blame the ratty sweater and faded jeans, or the day-old growth of beard, but she'd felt as if she could talk to him. That man was gone, replaced by a businessman in a charcoal-gray suit and a crisp shirt the color of his eyes. He dripped with wealth and power. Skycaps, attendants, security guards—they all straightened respectfully upon his approach. He moved through the terminal with entitled nonchalance, raincoat draped over his arm, wordlessly communicating to everyone that he was a man not just at one with his environment, but in command of it. A sexy prince, to the manor born.

When she boarded the jet, Emma could barely suppress her gasp of surprise. She wasn't sure what she'd expected, but it definitely wasn't this. The spacious cabin more resembled a living room than a plane. A nicer living room than her own, she noted, realizing it was the second time this week Kent family transportation outclassed her living space. In this case, she stood in an airborne version of a Kent hotel, complete with Oriental carpet and crystal light fixtures. Instead of seats, leather divans lined both sides, with a small table set in the back for conferencing. A heavy gray curtain blocked her view of the front, but through a gap in the material she glimpsed the stainless steel gleam of kitchen appliances.

"First time?"

"Excuse me?" Gideon's question broke the spell.

"Flying the Kent friendly skies. Is this your first time on the corporate jet?"

"It's very impressive."

"Beats domestic travel, that's for sure." He tossed his coat over the back of a divan and gestured for her to take a seat. "Make yourself comfortable, Miss O'Rourke. Or do you plan to stand the entire flight?"

Emma settled in across the aisle. The leather was so supple the seat molded to her instantly, like a glove. She tried to lean back and enjoy the sensation. A seat belt latch nudged her hip. She looked around for its companion. Was it too early to buckle up? Did she even have to?

Meanwhile, across the aisle, Gideon remained unrestrained and looking more at home amid the opulence than a man had a right to. He must have noticed her squirming, for he glanced at her curiously.

"Are you sure everything is all right?" he asked.

"Everything's *fi*—" She caught herself and sighed. This was going to be a long trip. Maybe she should ban his asking if she was all right. "Why wouldn't it be?"

He shrugged. "No reason. Except your spine is stiffer than a steel rod. You are allowed to relax, you know. This is a business trip, not a kidnapping."

"Thanks for clarifying."

"Just making sure you knew."

Before Emma could answer, a disembodied voice filled the cabin. "We'll be taxiing into position shortly, Mr. Kent. The weather's a bit choppy over Connecticut, so we might encounter a little turbulence."

Emma buckled her seat belt. From across

the aisle, she could feel Gideon watching. She tried to avoid the sensation by rummaging through her briefcase for reading material. Her insides were jittery enough without the added voltage that seemed to flare whenever she looked in his direction. It was as if her body had some kind of electrical switch when he was around. He only need move into her vicinity and her nerve endings got all twittery, disrupting her equilibrium.

The plane lurched forward, having begun its taxiing in earnest, and pitching Emma off balance in the process. She righted herself, using the shift in position to camouflage another tug on her seat belt.

"Did you bring the Silbermann file?" Gideon asked.

She looked up. Leaning back on the divan, legs stretched across the aisle, Gideon was the picture of comfort and ease. An incredibly handsome picture. She caught her breath as the inevitable charge passed through her. "Yes," she replied. He'd asked her to pack the design sketches when he'd arrived with Hinckley. "I've got them right here."

"Good. Let's take a look."

To her surprise, he crossed the aisle and

buckled himself into the seat next to hers. "You need to look at them, too."

"I do?"

"Didn't I say I expected you to give your opinion?"

"Yes, but—"

"So you might as well start now. What is it about these designs, exactly, that makes you think they're cold?"

Oh Lord, they were back to that, were they? "A tad moot, don't you think? Your grand-mother already approved the project."

"Humor me." He took the file from her hands and leafed through until he found a sketch of the suggested lobby refurb. "What don't you like about this one, for example?"

Emma stared at the drawing, trying her best to focus on design and not the thigh pressing against hers, or the seductive hint of limes and spice emanating from his skin. Talk about futile. Worse, she knew next to nothing about interior design. How on earth was she going to make an intelligent comment?

"Well?"

He wouldn't give up until she said some-thing. For whatever reason, he seemed hell-bent on getting her commentary.

"The color," she said finally. "I don't like the color."

"You don't like blue?"

Actually, no. She hated blue, navy especially. More so now that the color dominated her wardrobe. She didn't tell him, though. "It's the wrong shade," she said instead. "This blue is too harsh, too icy. It should be more…"

She looked up into Gideon's eyes, causing the rest of her sentence to die on her tongue. Maybe she didn't hate all blue….

"More what?" he asked.

"Brilliant."

Realizing what she'd just breathed, she jerked her gaze to her lap. "Not a very helpful suggestion, was it?"

"On the contrary, I understand perfectly."

"You do?" She couldn't help herself; she looked back up.

"Sure," Gideon replied. "Color evokes emotion. When speaking viscerally, you can't always name a shade."

"And here I thought I was simply verbally inept."

"I seriously doubt you're ever inept, Miss O'Rourke."

The compliment sparked more satisfaction

than it should. "Oh, you'd be surprised, Mr. Kent," she replied, deflecting the sensation. "I can be plenty inept when I put my mind to it."

"Further proving your efficiency. True ineptitude doesn't require effort. By the way," he added softly in her ear, his conspiratorial tone setting off a new batch of shivers, "we're in the air."

"What?" She looked out the window. Sure enough, Boston, along with the rest of New England, was rapidly receding from view. She'd been so distracted by Gideon, she hadn't noticed their liftoff.

Which had been the point, she realized. "How did you…?"

Gideon shrugged. "Lucky guess. Plus you had that seat belt of yours locked in a death grip." Emma blushed. "You don't like flying?"

"Actually, I don't know if I like flying or not. This is my first time. In fact…" if she was going to confess, she might as well admit everything "…I've never been farther than Providence."

"Huh."

Something about the way Gideon said that

one syllable unnerved her. Especially since he fell silent for the minute or so that followed. Was he regretting dragging her along? Worrying she might not know how to act in front of Ross Chamberlain? Normally she'd find such concerns insulting, but he looked so regal and elegant in comparison to her that suddenly she was worried about her ability to perform, as well.

She fiddled with the buckle on her seat belt, lifting the metal latch up and down. "See?" she said, breaking the awkward silence. "I told you I had areas of deficiency."

"Inexperience is hardly a deficiency. In fact—" he shrugged "—maybe it's a benefit. Really," he added when Emma scoffed. "You see things with a fresh perspective."

"Like cold interior design," she remarked self-deprecatingly.

"Don't forget comfortable beds."

The smile accompanying his reply shorted out her internal electrical switch. Her nerve endings flared. Covering the reaction, she peered into her briefcase. Thank goodness for business talk. "I printed out last year's correspondence with Mr. Chamberlain, along with some of the most recent news articles from the trades. I thought you might want them for background. Would you like to review them?"

"Later." Gideon was actually fishing through his own attaché. "Much as Mariah thinks otherwise, I do have a business of my own to run."

"Fishing charters."

He chuckled. "You've been listening to Mariah too much. Castaway Charters is a little more extensive than a fishing business. We do sailing vacations, island getaways, worldwide tours. Mariah makes it sound like I'm standing on the beach flagging down tourists."

"I'm surprised."

"What, that I'm not flagging down tourists?"

"That you didn't go into the hotel business. I would have assumed, what with growing up in the industry…"

A shadow crossed his face. "Yeah, well you know what they say about assuming."

She did, indeed, and she should have known better than to fall into the trap. Assumptions were as bad as fantasies. No good came out of either.

They spent the next half hour or so in

silence, Gideon engrossed by work, Emma trying not to think about the firmness of his shoulder pressed against hers. Now that they were in the air, she thought he might move back across the aisle, but he didn't. He remained buckled next to her, a large, silent, impossible to ignore presence. She cursed herself for not bringing work of her own along. She'd been so intent on gathering everything Gideon needed, not to mention stressing out about her first flight, that she forgot. Now, without the distraction, she was hyperfocusing on the unhealthy images she'd buried earlier.

Desperate to stop her train of thought before it got going, she pulled out her organizer and began writing unnecessary reminders on her to-do list. Silly things like "pick up trash bags" and "laundry" just so she'd have something to do.

Unfortunately, she ran out of items within a few minutes. It didn't take long before she traded staring at her calendar for stealing glances at the man next to her. Gideon was lost in his own thoughts and didn't notice. He stared off in the distance, absently tracing the tip of his gold pen along his lower lip. Emma felt a surge of envy, watching the pen go back and forth. He had a remarkably beautiful mouth.

What thoughts distracted him? she wondered. Something pleasurable, no doubt, for his features had relaxed, the tension erased from his jaw. Daydreaming looked good on him.

Everything looked good on him, she realized. The suit, the plane. Even that ratty sweater. *A prince to the manor born,* she repeated to herself. Which made her what?

The poor Little Match Girl. On a corporate jet, heading for Manhattan. She turned and checked the view from her window. The plane appeared to be descending; they were no longer above the clouds. Far off in the distance, she saw a cluster of buildings that had to be New York City.

She would never admit it out loud, but looking at those buildings, she felt a thrill passed down her spine.

She was heading to New York.

They had to be kidding. Andrew Kent wanted to renovate this place? As Gideon guided her through the Landmark lobby, Emma couldn't help swiveling her head like a tourist.

Everywhere she looked she saw something—a vase, a painting, a carving—that took her breath away. She'd always thought the Fairlane to be the height of luxury, but this place… With its gold embossed ceiling and dark red marble, she felt as if she'd walked into a palace.

Complete with a handsome prince.

"The ceiling is supposed to remind you of Cortez's lost city," Gideon said when she glanced upward. "In fact, this whole design has an Aztec motif. Very popular during the Art Deco period." He pointed behind her, to the large mosaic hanging above the main entrance, a swirling mass of color and motion. "That's Quetzalcoatl, the Aztec sky god."

"It's breathtaking," Emma replied.

"Yes, it is." His eyes were on her as he answered, making her stomach flutter. "Don't tell Mariah…" he leaned into her space, the upturned collar of his overcoat tickling her cheek "…but I think this place could rival the Fairlane."

"Careful, that's heresy," Emma replied, though she understood his point. "The Fairlane is more mainstream, more modern. This place has an…I don't know…an energy, maybe? I feel like I'm stepping back in time."

"Andrew would call that feeling dated."

"Maybe, but I like the look. It's—"

"Let me guess. Warm." He shot her a grin that, had he been anyone else, would have earned him a smack on the arm.

Emma blushed. "Are you teasing me?"

"Not at all. I'm agreeing with you. You have an eye for design, Miss O'Rourke. You should share your opinion with Mariah."

Hoping the color flooding her cheeks again wasn't too evident, Emma looked away. Gideon's words flattered her more than she wanted to admit. She'd never been told she had a flair for anything. Other than hard work, that is. To cover, she laughed them off. "I'm sure your uncle Andrew would love that."

"Andrew spends too much time listening to Suzanne."

"Who?"

"The latest wife. No doubt she's the one who pushed for Josh Silbermann in the first place."

"Oh." Emma knew who he meant. A statuesque blonde several years Andrew Kent's junior, she always dressed stunningly and never acknowledged Emma's existence. "Well, she is very stylish."

"Pretentious, Miss O'Rourke. The word you're looking for is *pretentious*. As well as superficial, hard to please and short-term. Andrew tends to like them that way.

"Sort of a Kent family tradition," he added with a wry smile.

Including him? Emma kicked herself for letting the thought cross her mind. Gideon's preference in women was none of her business. It wasn't as if she would make the list, anyway. In fact, she couldn't believe she was even entertaining the idea.

"I better go check on our rooms," she said, determinedly returning to business matters.

"No need. We've been spotted." He nodded toward a short, ruddy-faced man marching in their direction.

"Mr. Kent!" the man exclaimed in a clipped, semi-British accent. He clasped Gideon's hand in both of his. "Welcome back."

"Sebastian. You haven't changed a bit."

"Well, not so much that a little hair color won't hide, eh?"

"You have gray hair?"

"You should know. You caused most of it."

He turned and smiled at Emma. "You must be Miss O'Rourke. I see this rascal hasn't talked you into taking your shoes off yet."

"Why would I take my shoes off?" She looked at Gideon who, to her surprise, actually had color in his cheeks.

"One time, Sebastian," he replied. "That was one time. And the floors were freshly waxed. I couldn't help myself."

"He couldn't help himself with a lot of things. Gave his grandmother fits, he did. He and those cousins of his." Sebastian's smile grew serious. "It's good to have you home again, sir."

"Just a short visit, Sebastian. Nothing permanent."

"Of course." There was no mistaking the disappointment in the manager's voice. It was so evident that Emma felt disappointed herself. Everyone, it seemed, wanted Gideon to stay.

Breaking the silence, she turned to Sebastian. "I was just about to check on our rooms."

Like any good employee, he quickly righted himself. "Of course. Two suites, just as you requested."

No, not as she requested. She'd reserved one suite for Gideon and a standard room for herself. "Actually…" She paused, trying to think of a way to correct the situation without calling attention to the manager's mistake.

"Thank you, Sebastian. I knew I could count on you."

Emma frowned at Gideon. "You changed the reservations?"

"Last night, and before you ask why, I like having you close by.

"Don't worry," he added with a chuckle. He spoke just behind her ear, his breath tickling the hair on the nape of her neck. "The beds in the VIP suites are just as comfortable as the ones in the standard rooms. I promise."

Ten minutes later Emma stood in the middle of a parlor opulent enough to rival Mrs. Kent's. A VIP suite. What was Gideon thinking?

She looked around the living space, an elegant study in jewel tones and gold. There were three distinct areas. At one end, framed by a pair of floor-to-ceiling windows, a decorative fireplace flickered merrily, its flames complementing the darkening Manhattan skyline outside. Nearby sat a small dining table, perfect for a candlelit dinner.

At the other end was a large—no, make that a huge—conference table, wet bar and desk. Everything an executive would need for business.

Both orbited a third space, a cozy sitting area with a velvet sofa and matching Queen Anne chairs. For those in-between moments, she supposed, when the rich just wanted to relax and read the financials.

And all of this was contained in one of the three rooms. What was she doing here? What did Gideon expect her to do with so much space?

A soft cough drew her attention. A waspish man in a crisp red blazer hovered in the doorway. Her personal concierge, he explained when he arrived with the bellman. "Excuse me, madam. I had your luggage placed in the boudoir. Would you like me to call a maid to help you unpack?"

*A maid?* Emma blinked in surprise. What would the woman do, hang up Emma's one suit? "Thank you, but I can unpack myself," she replied.

"Very well, madam. My name is Robert. If

there's anything else you need, just ring the desk."

"I doubt I'll need anything. I'm only staying one night."

"Of course, madam."

The formality and courtesy unnerved her. Especially since it was unnecessary. Surely he recognized her hotel uniform?

"Excuse me, Robert," she called out as he was leaving.

He turned, his expression expectant. "Yes, madam?"

"Emma," she corrected. "There's no need to be formal. After all, we are both hotel employees, right?"

"Except you're staying in a VIP suite. And we've been given specific instructions to afford you every service and amenity."

"Instructed?" Emma wasn't quite sure she understood.

"By Mr. Kent. He made it quite clear when he called last night that you were to be treated as his special guest."

"He did?" Robert's answer unnerved her more than the solicitousness. Gideon had called her "special"? Why would he do that?

"Yes, ma'am. He said you were to be

exposed to every amenity the Landmark had to offer." The mask of indifference slipped slightly, and the concierge smiled kindly. "So I guess that makes you a little more than another hotel employee."

"No, I'm not," she said to herself after Robert left, more to quell the butterflies in her stomach than anything. She didn't know what Gideon was up to, but she wasn't sitting in a VIP suite because she was special. That was an idea her mother would fall for.

Emma wouldn't think about how enticing the idea sounded.

On her way back toward the corridor that divided the parlor from the rest of the suite, she stopped and studied her reflection in one of the mirrored doors. A pale, tired woman stared back. Not a woman who enchanted billionaire businessmen, but a woman who needed a nap.

Satisfied that she'd put Robert's comment well out of her head, she kicked off her heels and carried them through the boudoir into the bedroom. One thing was certain, she conceded as she entered the room. The bed did look comfortable. More than comfortable, it looked downright decadent. There had to be a dozen pillows, a literal sea of them, and the mattress seemed so high and thick she wondered if she wouldn't float away when she lay down.

She did so, and sure enough, a down topper enfolded her with softness.

"Wow, a girl could get used to this." She ran her hand across the damask duvet. The sapphire silk reminded her of the ocean.

Or Gideon's eyes.

Suddenly, the image of those eyes boring into her from above flashed through her brain, accompanied by a hot, needy quiver.

*Surely you have one or two fantasies....*

Her eyes flew open and she scrambled off the bed as if it were on fire.

This was her mother's fault. If she hadn't raised that ridiculous theory in the first place, Emma wouldn't be entertaining any of these thoughts. Foolish, inappropriate, completely unrealistic, waste-of-time thoughts. Gideon had booked her into this room because he wanted her nearby. For business reasons, nothing more. This suite, this trip—they were a onetime deal.

She was overtired. That was it. Strung out from nerves and new experiences. A hot shower—that's what she needed. Something to unwind her tense muscles.

Like everything else in the suite, the bathroom was spacious and luxuriously designed. The marble tub had to be the largest she'd ever seen. She'd never really been much of a bath person, mainly because she could never lounge comfortably. Her legs would stick out if she submerged her shoulders, and vice versa. Either way, she got cold. Plus baths were time-consuming; she usually had too much to do to indulge in them.

She had time now, though, didn't she? Their meeting wasn't until tomorrow afternoon, and Gideon….well, she imagined Gideon had friends in the city he wanted to spend time with.

And the tub was big. The size of a small swimming pool, really. She could lie down flat on the bottom and her toes still wouldn't touch the edge.

Why not? When was the next time she'd get an opportunity to swim in a tub? With bubbles, no less, she thought, grabbing a bottle from the vanity. Feeling silly and rebellious at the same time, she turned on the water and dumped the contents under the stream.

Seconds later the room filled with the sweet aroma of citrus and ylang-ylang.

She was just about to submerge her toes in the bubbles when a knock sounded on the door.

*Concierge Robert*, she thought with a sigh. He'd ignored her protest and sent a maid to unpack her things, anyway.

A large white robe hung on the back of the bathroom door. Throwing it on, Emma went to answer the door.

Only to wish she'd thought to use the peep-hole first.

# CHAPTER FIVE

"IS THIS A BAD TIME, Miss O'Rourke?"

It was Gideon, not the concierge, standing in her doorway. "I wanted to review the Chamberlain correspondence." His blue gaze raked her length, lingering, or so it seemed, on her belt. "Guess I should have called first."

When she didn't respond, he frowned. "Is everything all right?"

"Yes, I…" Emma shook coherent thought back into her head. "I wasn't expecting you."

"Obviously." His grin grew wider.

"I mean, I assumed you would have plans…."

"Ah, didn't your mother teach you about making assumptions?"

*In more ways than one,* thought Emma.

"Besides," he said, "why go out when I

can spend a stimulating evening reviewing financials with you? May I?"

He nodded toward her hallway. It took a moment for Emma to realize what he was asking; her head was stuck on his last comment. But eventually she stepped aside to let him pass. "Are you sure I'm not interrupting you?" he asked.

Emma thought of the lavender-filled bath growing cold. "No. Nothing important. My briefcase is in the bedroom. I'll go get it and meet you in the living room."

"Sounds good." He took two steps down the corridor, then turned. "Oh, and Miss O'Rourke?"

"Yes?"

"While you're in there, you might want to put something on under your robe. That belt doesn't tie very securely."

Emma gasped and clutched her collar. She didn't need a mirror to know her entire body had just turned crimson; the heat washing over her said as much. Holding the neckline tight, she dashed toward the bedroom, stopping halfway there when she realized her clothes were in the boudoir.

Check that; tomorrow's suit and her pajamas

were in the boudoir. The rest of her clothes lay on the bathroom floor. She turned back, grateful that the parlor was out of view. It was bad enough that she heard Gideon laughing to himself as she rushed off.

When she emerged a few moments later, still bare-legged but dressed, Gideon had already made himself at home. So at home that Emma had to catch her breath. He looked amazing. It was as if yesterday's sailor and today's prince had decided to merge, creating the perfect combination of casual sophistication. He'd shed his jacket and tie in favor of rolled-up shirtsleeves. Though the cotton garment had gone through a day's travel, on him it looked sharp as a tack. Even the five o'clock shadow on his cheeks was appealing. She glanced down at her uniform, wrinkled and not nearly as attractive looking, and self-consciously ran a palm across the front of her skirt.

He'd turned on the television and was clicking through stations with the remote. "I hope you don't mind, but I wanted to catch the market wrap-up." He looked up, saw her and frowned. "You didn't have to put your suit back on."

Instantly, her self-consciousness doubled. "Either that or my pajamas," she replied.

"You didn't pack anything else?"

Why would she? "I wasn't planning to stay more than tonight."

He made a clucking noise with his tongue. "We're going to have to do work on that practical streak of yours. Pajamas, by the way, aren't a problem if you'll be more comfortable."

"I wouldn't be."

"We'll have to work on that, too."

She wished he'd stop saying "we," as if they were a team. Every time he did, her stomach fluttered, and the sensation disturbed her. Especially after the thoughts she'd had earlier.

Curse her mother for putting those thoughts in her head.

There was a matching chair across from the sofa. Emma tucked herself in the corner and propped her briefcase on her lap like a shield. "Which would you like first, the correspondence or the figures."

"The fig— Damn, the Dow took another late-day tumble."

"A big one?"

"Big enough for me to appreciate being a

privately held company. Wonder how Kent Hotels did."

"I should think, being mostly privately held, the company did well enough. Unless someone impulsively decided to sell…" All the pieces suddenly slid into place. "That's why you're in New York, isn't it? Your grandmother is afraid Mr. Chamberlain will sell his stock, isn't she?"

"Ross has taken some big hits. Not to mention last year's very expensive divorce. Buzz on the streets says he's looking to shore up his liquid assets."

"And Mrs. Kent thinks he'll sell his Kent Hotel stock to do so."

"Exactly."

Emma paused, recalling what little she knew of the Kent-Chamberlain friendship. From the tone of Mrs. Kent's correspondence, the families had been friends for years. "Surely he wouldn't just sell, not without letting your grandmother know."

"Never underestimate the power of a greedy ex-wife breathing down a man's neck. Did you hear how worried Mariah was by a man called Gerard Ambiteau?"

Of course she had. "Your grandmother

makes me run news searches on the name every week."

"Glad to see the Internet's making Mariah's obsession easier. Ambiteau, or more specifically, Gerard Ambiteau, is Mariah's archenemy. Ever since he tried to buy Kent Hotels following Edward's death. He made the mistake of implying the hotel business was too much for a young widow with three children to handle."

"Ouch. Bet that went over well."

The smile Gideon flashed made Emma's toes curl. "About as well as a hydrogen bomb. Needless to say, Mariah took the offer as a personal affront. I swear she expanded the Kent empire as much to spite Gerard Ambiteau as anything."

"The ultimate revenge. Your grandmother's a formidable woman."

"Mariah's a survivor, that's for sure. Then again, married to Edward Kent, she'd have to be, right?"

Emma had heard the stories; Edward Kent's womanizing and debauchery were almost as legendary as his business acumen. "Surely it wasn't all bad," she said. "They did have three children."

"Ah yes, children, the ultimate indicator of true love." The bitterness in Gideon's voice made her shudder.

"Sorry," he quickly added. "I should learn to keep my cynical views to myself."

"That's all right. I understand what you're saying."

"You do?"

Was that surprise in his voice? "I was raised by a single mom, remember?" Emma of all people knew children weren't a guarantee of marital bliss.

Heck, few things were. She certainly knew of far more failures than successes. "Makes you wonder sometimes why people ever bother getting married in the first place."

"Exactly."

It was the succinct, definitive answer of a man whose mind was made up. Emma didn't know why, but her insides twisted at his decisiveness. Maybe it was the sudden change in atmosphere that followed. Gideon's cynical comments had caused him to fold into himself, taking the warmth from the room.

It was as if he were a human thermostat, Emma realized. When he was "present" the room pulsed. But as soon as he withdrew, the air grew cold, the coziness sucked away. It made her want to burrow next to him on the sofa and prod him teasingly until he returned.

However, since those actions were far too intimate and familiar for her to carry out, she settled for switching to a lighter subject. "How do you think your grandmother and Hinckley are getting along?"

Gideon didn't return completely, but his half laugh erased some of the fatigue from his face and brought back some of the warmth. "Right now I'm guessing they're arguing over who gets the bulk of the sofa."

"Wonder who will win."

"Hinckley, without question. When it comes to his comfort he's extremely stubborn. Mariah has met her match."

"Is that why she's cat-sitting?"

"Why, Miss O'Rourke, are you suggesting I foisted my spoiled, entitled, stubborn cat on Mariah as payback?"

"In a word, yes."

He pressed a hand to his chest. "I'm crushed that you could think such a thing. I was merely acting as any loving pet owner would, making sure my beloved cat was as comfortable as possible."

"My mistake. I apologize."

"She says while laughing."

Emma couldn't help it. His feigned indignation was so over the top, she had to. "Sorry," she repeated, trying to rein in her smile. She failed.

Earning herself a grin to beat all grins from the man across from her. A grin that not only brought back the warmth and coziness, but was bright enough to light Manhattan. Seeing it, Emma felt her insides tumble.

"I guess I can forgive you," he said. "But—" he pointed at her with the remote "—this means I get to choose the room service order."

"Wait a second. Your father sent an e-mail about that subject a few months ago…."

She was smart, that's for sure. Watching Emma search her laptop for a memo about Kent's overseas projects, Gideon couldn't help but be impressed. One mention of a figure and she could recall a document or memo, sometimes months old, referencing the conversation. Moreover, she had an intuitive ability to link content from one document to another seemingly unrelated one. No wonder Mariah was so keen on her secretary. Like with the hotel decor, the woman had a real feel for the business.

She was adorable, too. The way she stuck her nose in the computer, the tip of her tongue protruding in concentration... She'd relaxed enough to move from the chair to the floor, where she sat with her long legs curled like a cat's. Her shoes were off, and he could see her bare toes digging absentmindedly in the carpeting.

Again, adorable. He felt bad for letting his cynicism color the mood earlier. This atmosphere was far more pleasant.

"Here it is." Emma beamed with victory. "I knew I read those figures before. See?" She pivoted the computer screen so he could look. Sure enough, there was the memo outlining in great detail their upcoming Dubai project, including its impact on revenue.

"Management's very high on this new property," she said. Based on projected earnings, he could see why. "Of course, the numbers are still a few years out."

"True, but unlike a lot of investments, this

one promises to turn a profit fairly quickly."
He gave a quick nod of approval and turned
the screen back toward her. "Good call, Miss
O'Rourke. This might be exactly the carrot
we need."

"Just doing my job." She was trying to
sound nonchalant, but he caught a hint of pink
washing her cheeks.

"Is it your job to remember every detail of
every memo Kent Hotels has ever issued?"

"No, but with your grandmother, a good
memory helps."

"I suppose it does. Lord knows hers is long
enough. Mariah's lucky to have you, you
know."

"In this economy, I'm the lucky one. Good
jobs don't grow on trees."

"Don't sell yourself short. Mariah doesn't
sing praises easily, and she definitely sings
yours."

Another blush. Gideon leaned back against
the sofa, taking in the woman across from
him. For someone so competent, she sure
wasn't use to compliments. Hard to believe.
You'd think she'd be swimming in them.

"Have you ever thought of applying for a

management position? You have a nose for business."

She laughed, clearly deflecting the suggestion. "Down in the lobby you said it was an eye for design."

"So I did. Maybe you've got both, a nose and an eye."

"Goodness. I can't wait to find out if I have a mouth."

Oh, she did…a gorgeous one. It was Gideon's turn to look away as a half-dozen images, all of them inappropriate, popped into his head. That she seemed clueless to the innuendo made the remark all the more arousing. How on earth could a woman be so oblivious to her charms?

He pushed himself to his feet and moved to the window. Nighttime had claimed the sky, transforming the view into a study of shadows, shapes and light. After years of endless tropical horizons, he wasn't used to seeing buildings clustered so close together. It looked strange to him.

"What an amazing view."

Emma approached, her eyes wide as she gazed out at the skyline. "It's breathtaking."

"Absolutely." Though he wasn't thinking

about the view. Like this afternoon in the lobby, he found her expression far more captivating than his surroundings. Watching her made the male part of him flood with awareness. Forget sweet. She was *beyond* sweet. Why weren't there men lined up to spoil her?

Then again, maybe there were. Maybe there was a guy back in Boston spoiling her to death. For some reason Gideon found that idea unsettling. Probably because if there was a guy, he was doing a pretty poor job. A spoiled woman wouldn't blush at every compliment. Or lack expectations.

There were elements to Miss O'Rourke that just didn't line up.

"What building is that?"

Her question drew his attention. Emma had moved closer and was pointing to an angular structure a couple blocks away. She looked at Gideon expectantly.

"I'm not sure. The skyline's changed since my last visit. I think maybe a bank."

"Oh."

Dammit if he didn't feel he'd let her down. Determined to make up for it, he steered her by the shoulders until she stood in front of him. "Here," he said, "look to the left. That's the Chrysler Building."

He watched as she craned her neck to get a better view. Though he hadn't meant to, his maneuvering left her cradled against his chest. He could feel her body heat through his shirt. When he turned his own head to follow her gaze, his nose caught a hint of her vanilla-scented skin.

"You can't get views like this from the second floor," he said. It was taking all his self-restraint not to bury his nose in the curve of her neck and inhale.

"No, I don't suppose you can."

She smiled at him over her shoulder. A shy, half-lidded smile. *Bedroom eyes,* thought Gideon, his blood heating, *with bedroom lips to match.* So pink and luscious. He bet they tasted as sweet as everything else about her. All it would take was a little dip of his head…

"Would you like me to type up in one document what we discussed this evening?" Emma's voice suddenly dissolved the spell. "That way you can have all the figures in one place when you review them in the morning."

Breaking free of his orbit, she moved back to the center of the room, back to where their paperwork lay strewn across the coffee table.

Back to business.

Just as well, thought Gideon. He swallowed his sigh and straightened his shoulders. "Thank you, Miss O'Rourke. That would be very helpful."

Talk about making a fool of herself. After Gideon left, Emma slipped the dead bolt in place, then rested her forehead against the door. What had she been thinking? She'd come this close—*this close*—to kissing Gideon Kent! One second she was looking at the Chrysler Building, the next she was gazing into those beautiful blue eyes and drifting slowly toward them. Thank God rational thought had kicked in at the last minute. Before she'd completely embarrassed herself.

It was the suite, she decided. The opulence made her act like an idiot. Well, that and Gideon. He had this way of making her feel unnerved and relaxed at the same time. Not to mention he was gorgeous, funny, smart, sexy…

Listen to her; she was going on like her mother summing up a potential boyfriend. The man was her boss, for goodness sake! And after tomorrow he wouldn't even be that. He'd be wrapping up his visit and she'd be back to typing Mrs. Kent's correspondence.

Leaving the doorway, Emma padded into the bathroom. The robe lay on the floor where she'd discarded it, along with her stockings. She picked up the garment and returned it to the hook on the door. Then she sat down on the tub's edge. The water had long ago grown cold, the bubbles and lavender aroma dissolved. So much for indulging. Then again, maybe she'd indulged enough for one night.

She unplugged the drain and headed back to the parlor.

*She wore an evening dress. The kind princesses wore. Her shoulders were bare. A muscled torso pressed against her back; hot breath sounded in her ear. She sighed as strong hands caressed her shoulders. "Show me your fantasies, Miss O'Rourke...."*

The sound of ascending chimes cut through Emma's dream and her eyes flew open. What the—?

Her phone. It was ringing. Blinking in the darkness, she groped along her nightstand, telling herself her rapid breathing was from being startled awake, not from the dream she'd been having.

"Hey, sweetie, how's New York?" Her mother's high-pitched voice bellowed from the other end. "Mary and I are on our way home so we thought we'd see how you were doing. We're not interrupting anything, are we?"

"Huh? No. I'm in bed."

"And?"

It took her a moment to realize what her mother meant. "No!" Emma repeated vehemently. "I told you, Mom, this is a business trip."

"What, you don't think men like to combine business with pleasure?"

Flashes of her dream popped into Emma's mind. She shook them off, replacing them with Gideon's gentlemanly departure last night. "Not Gideon."

"Ooh, Gideon, is it?"

"Mom, he's my boss. Quit trying to imply something else." *Quit putting stupid thoughts in my head,* was what she really meant.

Out of the corner of her eye she noticed the clock on the nightstand, and something her mother had said clicked. "Did you say you were on your way home? It's five-thirty in the morning. Were you at the casino all night?"

"What can I say? We met some new friends and time got away from us."

There was the sound of giggling on the other end and Emma winced. Not again. "What's his name?" she asked, settling in for the usual download of information.

"Tony, and he's absolutely amazing. He's got a house on the Cape. And a boat. We're going to have the best time this summer. Maybe you can join us."

"Sure, sounds fun," Emma replied flatly. Inwardly, she sighed.

Her mother was talking rapidly now, clearly on a high from last night's "friendship." She'd be living on enthusiasm and coffee for the next couple of days. Until she either drove this Tony person away or he got bored and stopped calling. Then it would be days of bitterness and depression.

"And not one of those little fishing boats, either. This one sleeps five people, and you can water-ski behind it." Prattling on, mostly about Tony and how wonderful he was, Janet didn't even notice her daughter's silence. "We're meeting him and his friend Jimmy at the Prudential for drinks later today. As soon as we've had a chance to go home and change, that is."

Guess looking for work was out this week. Her mother would be far too busy hitching her wagon to Tony from the Cape. Life would be so much easier if her mom would just see it a little more realistically.

*Like you were doing last night?* a voice in Emma's head asked.

"Yes," she answered back. Because unlike her mother, she caught herself before the foolish ideas took hold.

And besides, even if she did do something stupid, which was highly unlikely, she was smart enough not to pretend there was a fairy tale ending on her horizon.

## CHAPTER SIX

"Wow, Ross Chamberlain sure knows how to talk. Too bad he doesn't say anything interesting. No wonder his wife wanted out. She probably feared being bored to death."

Speaking as he went, Gideon strode into Emma's suite ahead of her, not waiting for an invitation. They were back from their meeting, and rehashing what had transpired. It turned out Mrs. Kent's worries were well founded. Gerard Ambiteau had put out a few feelers, hinting that with her getting on in years, Kent Hotels might not be such a solid investment for a man with financial constraints.

Fortunately, Gideon had managed to persuade Chamberlain, through numbers and more than a little personal charm, to honor their families' long history. Emma was still a little breathless from the display. He'd been a sight to behold, a heat-seeking missile exuding charisma and business acumen. Ross Chamberlain never stood a chance.

"Should we call your grandmother and tell her the good news?" she asked.

"Later. First I say we toast our success." He made a beeline for the bar by the windows.

Emma watched in puzzlement as he uncorked a cut glass carafe and poured himself a drink. With his business concluded, she was surprised Gideon wasn't in more of a hurry to get his things and leave. By her calculations they could be back in Boston within a few hours. She certainly didn't understand why he was making himself at home in her suite.

"Join me?" he asked.

She shook her head. "I'm not much of a whiskey drinker."

"The bar's fully stocked."

"Then maybe a bottled water."

He rolled his eyes and tossed her one of the plastic bottles lined up by the ice chest. "Really, Miss O'Rourke, we have to work on your relaxation skills."

"Sue me, I like to stay hydrated."

"Is that what you call it," he teased, with a smile that curled her toes. Then he raised his glass. "To us."

"To keeping the wolf at bay," Emma retorted.

"For now, at least."

"What do you mean? I thought Mr. Chamberlain was fully on board." That sure seemed to be the case when they'd left him.

"Oh, he is, but I'm afraid we've only plugged a small leak. There's still the bigger question of when Mariah steps down. Andrew's reputation as a manager is shaky. He's made more than a few questionable decisions. Especially lately." Although Gideon didn't say so, the words *since he married Suzanne* came through loud and clear.

"What about your father?" From the way the brothers met with Mrs. Kent in tandem, she assumed they ran Kent Hotels the same way. "Surely his reputation is solid."

"Oh, definitely. Jonathan has an impeccable reputation. He's very good at presenting what people want to see." Gideon didn't even try to hide the edge in his voice. It was so sharp, Emma could feel it on the other side of the room. "Unfortunately, he's not very good 'when the rubber hits the road,' as the saying goes."

Watching Gideon toss back his drink, she

thought, not for the first time, that his comments must refer to more than the family business. "What do you think they'll do?"

"Short of Mariah living forever, which—" he jabbed the air with his index finger "—isn't out of the realm of possibility, I don't know. Her grand plan certainly didn't work."

"Grand plan?"

"Nothing. Just something between her and me. It doesn't matter."

He was folding into himself again, and the air chilled as a result. Without waiting for him to ask, Emma approached the love seat, slipped the glass from his fingers and refilled it. Blue eyes met hers as he accepted the drink. With a whoosh, the chill disappeared and the air began to crackle with a kind of tense heat. She wondered if Gideon noticed the change, as well, for he cleared his throat before taking a sip.

Needing to break up the atmosphere, she reached for the hotel phone and a safe topic. "What time would you like me to have the driver bring the car around?"

"Why? In a hurry to leave?" Gideon asked.

"No. I mean, I'm fine." He arched a brow

and she stopped. Apparently the word ban was still in place. "It's just that we've done our business in the city, and I didn't think you wanted to spend more time here than necessary."

"I appreciate the consideration," he replied. "But what about you?"

"What about me?"

"You didn't get to see many sights during your first trip to New York."

"I'll live. Besides, what I did see was great. The view from the window…" A flash from her dream popped into her head. She took a quick drink from her water to cover her flush.

Fortunately, Gideon didn't notice, as he was too intent on arguing his point. "A hotel view and a couple of car rides hardly count as 'seeing the city.'"

"Oh, well. Maybe next time."

"Hmmm, next time." He frowned and disappeared into his thoughts for several seconds before abruptly draining his drink and slapping the empty glass on the coffee table. "I've got it," he said. "Go change."

"Change?" She wasn't sure what he meant.

"Into your evening clothes. I'm taking

you out for the quintessential New York experience."

"Excuse me?" Emma took another drink to drown the butterflies Gideon's suggestion released in her stomach. Surely she misunderstood. "Did you say go out?"

"Yes, for dinner. To celebrate today's success, and to show you more of the New York than a window view. What do you say?"

What did she say? Emma didn't know what to say. Dinner with Gideon? The idea was… well, it was…

"It's not necessary," she replied.

"Why not? You've earned it. I wouldn't have been able to pull off today without your input. Your background knowledge was invaluable. And that report was fantastic."

She blushed. "All I did was merge a few files."

"You did a lot more than that." When she blushed again, he chuckled under his breath. "What's the matter, Miss O'Rourke, afraid you might enjoy seeing the city with me?"

"No!" The protest came out far quicker than she intended. "I mean, yes, I would love to see New York." Especially with him. Which was why she hesitated. His proposal sounded too good to be true. "I don't want you to delay your return to Boston to take me sightseeing, though."

"Even if I want to?"

He wanted to? The butterflies took flight again. "But your grandmother…"

"Mariah can wait twenty-four hours. Now go change."

Emma looked down at her gray wool skirt with its coordinating black turtleneck, the only nonuniform outfit she had, and winced. "I can't."

"What do you mean you— Oh that's right, you didn't pack other clothes." He let out a long breath. "I swear, you must be the only woman on the planet who packs light."

"I didn't plan on taking a sightseeing tour," she said with a sheepish shrug. "But no worries. I don't have to change."

"I wouldn't want you to," he said, in a voice so low its timbre hummed through her. "Not one bit."

He meant her outfit, right? The way he looked at her, with his eyes heavy-lidded and unreadable, it would be easy to assume something else.

*Ah, but didn't he warn you about assuming…?*

"Besides—" she covered her thoughts with a laugh "—isn't the quintessential New York experience a hot dog in Central Park? Hardly necessary to dress up for that, right?"

"I had a slightly different experience planned."

Like what? she wondered, fighting the urge to speculate. "Sorry I ruined your plans."

"Who says they're ruined? Just go downstairs to the boutique and find something to wear."

His matter-of-fact answer made Emma laugh. She'd seen this "boutique." A tiny designer enclave off the lobby with accessories that cost more than her weekly paycheck. "How about I stick to my suit and we get the hot dog," she replied.

"Miss O'Rourke…" Gideon's eyes narrowed; she was about to get reprimanded.

"Really, Mr. Kent. A hot dog in the park sounds terrific." And cheaper. She wasn't about to max out her credit card on some designer dress no matter how tempting the idea of dinner sounded. Her mother splurged enough for both of them. Emma couldn't afford to fall down the same slippery slope.

"In fact," she continued, "I'm so hungry I might eat two hot dogs. With cheese and chili. Just let me get my bag."

"Miss O'Rourke." As she started past, he gently grabbed her arm. "You know that I meant for you to charge the dress to the room, right?"

No, she did not. Emma looked to the ground, embarrassed that she hadn't understood what he was saying. Now that she did, her head was spinning. He'd offered to buy her a dress? "I can't do that."

"Why not?"

"Because." Because it was too surreal. He'd already booked her into a luxury suite, flown her in a private jet. Things like this just didn't happen to her.

"Consider it a bonus for a job well done," he said, cutting her off. "I meant what I said before. I wouldn't have pulled off today's meeting without you. And don't say you were just doing your job."

"I don't need a bonus." Really, it was bad enough that his compliments were making her head spin.

"No one needs a bonus, Miss O'Rourke. But you do deserve one."

She shook her head. "Really, I—"

"Hey, Emma." He caught her chin, stopping the protest. "Let someone do something nice for you."

When had he closed the space between them? With him standing near her this way, his body teasing the boundaries of her personal space, she couldn't think sensibly. She got too lost in the combination of his body warmth and unique scent.

"Go to the boutique," he said in a low voice. "Indulge yourself. I insist." His set expression told her he wasn't about to stop insisting, either.

Looking into his eyes, now the color of a stormy sky, Emma felt her resolve fade away. Well, now she knew how Ross Chamberlain felt. A person didn't stand a chance when Gideon locked you into his sights.

The boutique, called Christine's, was empty and about to close when Emma got to the lobby. Even so, a stunning blonde with perfect posture greeted her at the door as if she was the first customer of the day. "Miss O'Rourke," she said with a smile, "I'm Christine. Mr. Kent said you were on the way down. You're looking for a cocktail dress?"

"Nothing too fancy," Emma replied. Once out of Gideon's mind-altering presence, she'd regained her senses, making up her mind that while she was going to buy a new dress, she'd pay for it herself. Her credit card didn't need the charge, but she would feel more in control. Something that seemed to be rapidly disappearing during this trip. "I'd like to wear it more than once."

"One little black dress coming right up," Christine replied. She led Emma toward the rear of the store. As they passed a rack of brightly colored party dresses, Emma felt a stir of longing. They all looked so vibrant and alive.

*Be practical*, she told herself. If she was going to spend a lot of money, she should buy an investment piece, not a trendy swath of silk.

Meanwhile, Christine was pulling back the curtain in a large dressing area. "I took the liberty of selecting a few outfits you might like," she said, "If none of these suit your taste, we can keep looking."

A dozen dresses of various styles, lengths and colors lined the wall. Emma fingered a beaded jacket sleeve. "How did you know my size?"

The look she received in response was simultaneously knowing and discreet. *Gideon.* A thrill buzzed through her at the idea that he'd studied her figure. And studied quite accurately, she realized, looking at the size.

"As I said," Christine continued, "these are only a few suggestions. We have others, as well."

"I'm sure one of these will be fine." Emma couldn't help noticing that none of the dresses had price tags. Not a good sign.

*Investment,* she repeated. Investment. She held up a black crepe sheath. The little black dress of little black dresses.

"That's the perfect investment dress," Christine said, reading her mind. "You could wear it for years and never be out of style."

Couldn't get more practical than that, could you? Or duller, she thought, turning the garment from front to back. Plain, simple, shapeless but not too shapeless. Switch the black to navy blue and you'd have her uniform.

"You can always dress it up with accessories," Christine offered.

Sure, she could. Scarves, jewelry. Emma knew all the tricks, thanks to the other women at work. They never really worked, though. In the end, you still wore a plain, simple dress. On the other hand, she was already wearing matching shoes, which would cut down on expenses, and she knew she could wear the style. If the dress fit, it was the right choice.

Maybe once she tried it on, she'd feel more positive.

She was halfway out of her turtleneck when a flash of color caught her eye, stopping her in her tracks. There, hanging on the discard rack, was the most brilliantly blue dress she'd ever seen. Sleek and sexy, the satin material shone under the track lighting, reminding her of Gideon's eyes. Maybe that's why she lifted it from the rack.

"Oh, that dress is one of my favorites," Christine said. "Isn't the color magnificent?"

Still thinking of Gideon's eyes, Emma replied, "Gorgeous." Hypnotic even, the way the garment called to her.

"I know you wanted a little black dress, but

your hair and coloring would be perfect with this shade. You really should try it on."

"I don't think so." She couldn't. The gown was way too impractical. She would never wear the thing after tonight. In fact, it was probably too fancy for tonight. "I should stick to basic black." Dull, serviceable basic black.

"Are you sure? The dress is your size. Maybe fate's trying to send you a message."

"Yeah, right."

"Why don't you try it on for fun," Christine prodded. "You don't have to buy it."

Emma knew what the saleswoman was trying to do. She'd noticed Emma's hesitancy and was now trying to sway her to what was obviously a more expensive item.

Still, the dress was extraordinary. She fingered a cap sleeve. The material glided beneath her fingers, smooth as ice. She bet it would feel amazing on a person's skin. A longing, fierce and sudden, welled up inside her.

*Go on,* a voice whispered in her head. *You know you want to.*

What the heck. She already knew she was buying the black crepe. When was the next time she'd get to try on an unspeakably expensive designer dress? Why not have a little fun? The color would probably look awful on her, anyway. Saleswomen always told you what you wanted to hear.

A soft rustle filled the room as she stepped into the dress. She'd been right; the satin did feel amazing. After slipping on one sleeve, then the other, Emma zipped the side and looked in the mirror, expecting to discover the dress was too tight or too misshapen or woefully garish against her skin. Instead, she gasped. Behind her, Christine gasped as well.

The dress fitted perfectly. The modest neckline showed a hint of cleavage, while the back draped nearly to her waist, revealing a sexy expanse of creamy skin. The skirt skimmed her hips perfectly, almost too perfectly, revealing lines and curves she didn't know she had. Surely this body wasn't hers.

"Don't move," Christine said. She drew closer. "Do you mind if I do something?"

Before Emma could reply—not that she could speak at the moment, since her reflection had her too stunned—the woman pulled the hairclip from Emma's hair. Her copper-colored locks spilled around her shoulders, but only briefly before Christine swept it back in a kind of semi chignon.

"This dress calls for a more sophisticated updo," she said. A small change, but a stunning one nonetheless. Emma blinked, transfixed by the transformation.

"And shoes," she heard Christine saying. She disappeared into the main store and returned with a pair of silver sandals. "Here, put these on."

Still stuck in her trance, Emma obeyed. The heels were higher and strappier than she'd normally wear, but they suited the dress perfectly. For the first time in her life, Emma didn't mind the endless stretch of leg.

"Still think you should stick to basic black? That dress was made for you," Christine said. "I told you, fate was giving you a message."

"You think?" She still couldn't believe her reflection. Who knew one dress could make such a difference? With the hair and the shoes, she felt like a celebrity.

Or a princess.

She looked at the crepe dress waiting on its hanger. This dress probably cost more than she made in a month. The black was the best choice. The practical choice. The responsible choice. Her gaze flickered back to her reflection.

"I'll take this one." The words shot from her mouth unbidden. The moment she said them, her nerves began to tingle. What was she doing?

Christine didn't give her a chance to change her mind. "Great," she gushed. If Emma didn't know better, she'd swear the woman was genuinely excited about her choice. "Now, let's touch up your makeup."

Fifteen whirlwind minutes later, Emma had become a different person. Christine didn't so much "touch up" her makeup as make her over. Her eyes were turned sultry and exotic. Crystal earrings dangled from her lobes, catching the light. Throughout it all, Emma felt lost, as if she were watching herself in a dream. A wild, unimaginable dream.

"Perfect," Christine said when Emma finally stepped from the dressing room. She looked over her shoulder for affirmation. "Don't you agree?"

"More than perfect." Gideon stood leaning against the counter, raw appreciation lighting his eyes. "Breathtaking."

The bottom fell out of Emma's stomach.

He handed her a heavy knit shawl that wasn't hers, but complimented the dress. Emma was too focused on his seductive gaze to protest. "Shall we?" he asked.

Feeling as if she were floating on air, she took his arm and let him lead her away.

The floating sensation stayed with her through the lobby and onto the street. While they'd been inside, the city had been shifting gears from business to social. Even though the sun was disappearing, its heat continued radiating from the pavement and buildings, keeping the air warm. Emma took in a deep breath, reveling in the encroaching summer night. After days of cold and gloom in Boston, the reprise felt wonderful.

"Is the restaurant very far?" she asked.

Gideon shook his head. "No. Why?"

"I was wondering if we could walk a little. The warm air feels good."

Smiling, he guided her past the doorman. "We can do whatever you want." His palm skimmed the small of her back, and the spark running up her spine made her feel so alive she could have run a marathon in her high heels. "Tonight's your night."

*Her night.* Her insides did a foolish little dance. Slipping her arm free from his, she pointed at the buildings lining the horizon. "Nice to finally see the top of the skyscrapers, isn't it?"

"Yeah, goodness knows you don't get to see that every day in downtown Boston."

She responded to his sarcasm with a smirk and a slight push to his shoulder. "Seriously, it's nice to see the sky change colors behind the buildings. All the different shades of pink and gray. Looks like a painting."

"Why, Miss O'Rourke, that sounds almost whimsical. Careful, whimsy's one step away from fantasy, you know."

"A momentary slip, I assure you," she replied with a laugh.

"Oh, I hope not. I'd like to think we've awaken a sleeping giant. Emma O'Rourke, dreamer."

"Afraid not." She fiddled with her wrap. There'd been a honeyed note in his voice that made her nerves hum with an uncomfortable awareness. "I suppose these sunsets pale compared to what you're used to seeing," she said, changing the subject.

"A little. In Cabo San Lucas, there's this

place called Land's End where the sun literally drops off the edge of the world. You'd swear you were watching a big red ball sink into the water."

"Why, Mr. Kent, that sounds almost whimsical." She earned herself a smile and a salute.

They paused at an intersection to let a taxi pass. "There are days when I wouldn't mind sailing off into the sunset," she told him.

"Why don't you?"

"What, and leave all Kent Hotels has to offer?"

Her attempt at offhandedness failed. The look Gideon gave her was unsettling at best. "Seriously, why not?"

"Not everyone can take off. Someone has to stay and work."

"Who decided that someone had to be you?"

*Life did,* thought Emma. "Because that's the way it's always been," she said softly.

Somberness followed her answer. "Not tonight," Gideon replied in an equally low voice. "Not tonight.

They walked on in silence. Emma welcomed the respite. Following his words, she felt more aware of Gideon than ever. Every look, every movement registered in high definition on her brain. Like the way his sleeve brushed against her arm as they walked. Or how his fingers hovered oh so near hers, touching but not touching. A miniscule shift to the left would break contact, but she couldn't bring herself to move.

Instead, she stole a glance at his profile. If Gideon noticed, his expression didn't indicate. He stared ahead, his eyes focused on a point somewhere in the distance, as if scanning the horizon. Recalling those tropical sunsets, perhaps?

"You must be looking forward to going back."

He glanced at her, his muzzy expression that of a man yanked from his thoughts. "To Saint Martin," she added. Or Cabo, or whatever locale had dragged his thoughts away. "With your 'errand' complete, you'll be able to go home soon."

"Mmmm," he replied. "I suppose so."

She was surprised how much his answer disappointed her. What did she expect him to say?

Quickly, she changed the subject before the

emotion could take hold. "I have to admit I'm getting hungry. I don't suppose I can get a hint as to where we're going for dinner? Since you're not buying me a hot dog, that is."

"Nope. You'll have to wait and be surprised. We're only a few blocks away now. And I promise, you'll like it just as much as a hot dog."

"Promise? Because I happen to really like chili-cheese dogs."

Immediately, she regretted her teasing tone, because the smile Gideon flashed back was beyond sexy. As was is his voice. "I promise, Miss O'Rourke. This will be a dinner you'll never forget."

Gideon didn't know why he'd picked this particular restaurant. He'd never eaten here himself, having always considered the place a five-star tourist trap. But as soon as the elevator doors opened and he heard Emma's gasp, he knew he'd made the right decision. Thirty-five stories above Manhattan, the entire penthouse dining room was a glassed-in paradise. Outside, the skyline beckoned from all four sides. Inside, crystal chandeliers bathed the room in light softer than candles, while real flames adorned glass-topped tables. "Like dining in midair," the restaurant ads touted.

Manufactured romance, Gideon had always thought, but seeing the wonder on Emma's face, worth the effort. Her eyes danced, they sparkled so brightly. Pleasure shot from his head to his toes. Not sexual pleasure, but the thrill of having pleased her. Her lack of pretense fed his desire to treat her like a princess. The more she refused to indulge herself, the more he wanted to shower indulgence on her. He thought back to her earlier comment, about being the one to stay back and work. He wished he knew who or what had convinced her she couldn't have more.

"What do you think?" he asked, slipping the wrap from her shoulders. "Better than a hot dog?" Her speechless nod only made his satisfaction swell more, and compelled him to lean in closer. "Wait till you see the view up close."

Just then the maître d' approached them, a crisp, slim man in a silk suit. "May I help you?" he asked in a clipped voice.

Gideon introduced himself, and the man instantly snapped to attention. "Yes, of course, Mr. Kent. Right this way. Your table's waiting."

He led them through the crowded dining room to a table in the back with an unobstructed view of the Chrysler Building, just as Gideon had requested. A bottle of champagne was chilling in a nearby stand, also as he'd requested. Gideon waited until Emma had been seated, then slipped a generous tip in the man's palm. Normally he detested men who threw money and entitlement around, but tonight he made an exception. He wanted Emma to have an experience she wouldn't forget.

"Okay, I admit, this is better than a hot dog," she said once the maître d' had left them. "This view is beautiful."

Emma's eyes sparkled in the candlelight. He hadn't noticed before, but the brown had flecks of green. It made them glitter even more than usual. A man could get lost studying those eyes.

And that dress… Christine had outdone herself. He'd sent her a Little Match Girl and got a copper-haired siren. When Emma stepped from the dressing room, every ounce of air had rushed from Gideon's lungs and he was still having trouble getting it back. The woman sitting across from him wasn't his adorable Miss O'Rourke; she was a woman who swept coherent thought straight from a man's head.

"Not as beautiful as you."

He probably shouldn't have said the words aloud, but when her blush seeped past her collarbone, regret faded in favor of his growing arousal.

Arousal that kicked up a notch when she looked away and began fiddling with her silverware. He watched her set and reset the angle of her salad fork a half-dozen times. The woman honestly didn't know her own appeal, he realized. The stirring in his blood grew stronger.

Their waiter arrived and poured the champagne. When he departed, Gideon raised his glass. "To a memorable trip," he said.

"To keeping the wolf at bay," she replied, repeating her toast from earlier. He noticed her hand shook as she raised the glass to her lips.

"You're not nervous, are you, Miss O'Rourke?"

Another blush colored her cheeks. "A little,

maybe. This is all so different for me. I feel like everyone in the room's staring at me."

With that dress, they probably were, thought Gideon.

She swiveled the stem of her flute between her fingers. "It's like I have a gigantic O on my forehead for Out Of Place."

"Everyone feels out of place a little when they visit somewhere for the first time."

"Right. Even you?"

"Even me."

He reached across the table and squeezed her hand. A mistake, because Emma's eyes immediately darkened with awareness, sending his arousal into overload. It was all he could do not to raise her wrist to his lips and trail kisses up the inside of her arm until those eyes darkened to black.

Abruptly, perhaps because she could read his intention, she pulled her hand away. The motion was so quick Gideon nearly knocked over his champagne. By the time he recovered, she'd tucked both hands onto her lap. Out of his reach.

Dammit.

"Have you traveled to a lot of places?" From

the way she chewed her lip, he guessed she was trying to change the atmosphere.

"Depends upon what you consider a lot," he replied, obliging her. "Not nearly as much as you think. The larger my company gets, the more I seem to stay in one place. The irony of the hospitality industry."

"How large is your company?"

"We opened an Australian office last year, and next spring I'm setting up shop in the Pacific Northwest. That'll make…" he tallied the number in his head "…thirteen locations worldwide."

"Wow," she replied, "definitely not a fishing charter business."

He felt himself smile like an idiot at her impressed tone. "No, definitely not. Though it did start out as one."

"Really?"

He nodded and sipped his drink. Thanks to the champagne, and the whiskey he'd had earlier, he was feeling quite mellow. The personal history tripped off his tongue easily. "When I first arrived in the Caribbean, I didn't have a dime, so I had to work the boats to make a living. Eventually, I saved up enough to buy a boat of my own. One boat became two. The rest naturally followed."

"You're being modest. If it were that easy, every fisherman would be a millionaire." She leaned forward, chin cupped in her hand, face rapt with interest. "No wonder your grandmother wants you to take over Kent Hotels."

She bit her lip and quickly looked down at her place setting. "Sorry. I probably shouldn't have said that."

Embarrassment looked so cute on her. "You figured out Mariah's grand plan, did you?"

"Wasn't hard. Mrs. Kent said a couple things. Then there was the summons home, the visit to Mr. Chamberlain. Doesn't take a rocket scientist to connect the dots."

"I suppose not. Then again, Mariah never believed in subtlety, either."

"She doesn't have to. People do what she asks regardless."

"Gee, and what makes you say that?" Gideon teased.

"Oh, I don't know, this trip to New York maybe?" she teased back.

They grinned at each other, enjoying the shared joke for a couple seconds in silence. There were times, thought Gideon, when he felt he and Miss O'Rourke were reading the same page. Like two peas in a pod. Though her pea was by far the more delectable of the two. He studied the way she raised her glass to her mouth, appreciating how the liquid made her lips glisten. "You're curious," he said, guessing at her thoughts. "About why I don't want the job."

"Family politics is none of my business," she replied. "Besides, I would think you have your hands full running your own company."

"Nice to see someone at Kent Hotels recognizes that fact."

Curiosity continued to lurk in her eyes, but she said nothing. Nor would she, he realized gratefully. She would never push. The knowledge made him feel closer to her than he'd felt toward another person in a long, long time, and for a wild second he considered sharing his true reason for walking away from Kent Hotels. What would she say then? he wondered. To learn he wasn't really a Kent?

A voice in the back of his brain said she wouldn't care nearly as much as he did.

"Mariah will have to find someone else." While he spoke, he reached for the champagne and refilled their glasses. "Last time I looked, there were more than enough Kents to choose from. Andrew's son, Alexander, for example."

A slight frown crossed her pretty face.

"You have a problem with Alexander?" Gideon asked.

"I don't know Alexander."

"Then what?" He didn't like that her smile disappeared. He wanted it back.

"Nothing."

Not nothing. Something. Her dismissal made him all the more curious. Unlike her, he would press. "Miss O'Rourke, I thought when we left Boston, we decided you would share your opinions."

"About hotel business," she reminded him. "Not Kent family business."

"When it comes to the Kents, family business and hotel business are one and the same. Besides, call me quirky, but I like it when you speak your mind. Now, what bothers you about Alexander?"

"Nothing. I told you, I don't even know Alexander Kent."

"Yet you frowned when I mentioned his name. Why?"

"Well…" She went back to playing with

her flatware, obviously searching for a diplomatic response. "I couldn't help noticing you refer to your family in the third person. It's always 'Mariah' or 'Andrew.' You never say 'Grandmother' or 'Uncle.'"

"Would you own up to Andrew as your uncle?"

To his relief, she laughed. "If only we could choose our relations," she said. "Life would be so much easier, wouldn't it." It was a statement, not a question.

Tightness gripped Gideon's chest. *She understood.* He could see the understanding reflected in those luminous brown eyes. How she knew, he couldn't say, but she did, and the realization was more intoxicating than all her beauty and sweetness combined.

He wanted to grab her and pull her into his arms then and there. Instead, he raised his glass, silently toasting her as he drank. "Wouldn't it, though," he said. "Wouldn't it."

Emma had fallen down the rabbit's hole. Sitting in this glass tower, surrounded by the night, she'd been dropped in a different world. A beautiful, magical world of sparkling light.

She smiled at the man across the table. He smiled back, and her insides danced. There was magic in the way Gideon looked at her tonight, as well. It was as if every glance set off a flume of bubbles that started at her toes and floated to her brain, making her feel lighter than air. It certainly wasn't how a secretary should feel when eating with her boss; in the morning she would be kicking herself for getting carried away. But at the moment, with Gideon's eyes beckoning invitingly, she couldn't resist.

He was as perfect a dinner companion as she could imagine. While the waiter brought one gourmet treat after another, Gideon entertained her with stories of life in the Caribbean and the eccentric travelers that crossed his path. With each tale, her enchantment grew stronger. The rest of the dining room faded away until she wasn't aware of anything but Gideon. She studied the graceful way his fingers held the handle of his knife, watched the curve of his mouth as he laughed, with new, acute awareness, enjoying what seemed to be their own candlelit world.

Unfortunately, like all fantasies, dinner ended. While the elevator brought them back to earth, Emma closed her eyes, savoring the last few moments. When she opened them, she saw Gideon watching her with a curious smile.

"What?" she asked, shyness sweeping over her.

"Nothing," he replied, still smiling.

They walked outside to discover the city's second life in full swing. Neon lights threw colored patterns on the sidewalk, and high-heeled pedestrians replaced the commuter traffic. In silent agreement, Emma and Gideon began walking back to the hotel. Remnants of dinner's magic followed.

After a few feet, she turned to him. "Thank you. That was…" Words failed her.

No matter. Gideon seemed to understand, for he smiled. "I couldn't take you to New York and fail to show you anything but the inside of a hotel room, now could I?"

The innuendo in his words did nothing to quell the pull she was feeling toward him. "Still," she replied, "there's dinner and there's…this. All of it. The restaurant, the dress— Oh my God, the dress!" She clapped a hand to her mouth. "I forgot to pay!" She'd been so enchanted by her transformation she'd forgotten.

"Relax. When I called the boutique, I told Christine to charge everything to the room. I had a feeling you'd ignore my request."

Emma blushed. "Am I that predictable?"

"Afraid so."

"You didn't have to pick up the bill."

"I know. I wanted to. You deserved it. You deserved this whole night."

There was such tenderness in his voice, Emma felt herself falling. Perspective was getting harder and harder to keep. "For a job well done," she said.

"Because I wanted to," he replied again, reaching for her.

A gasp escaped her lips as the back of his fingers brushed her cheek. She looked up, saw the earnestness of his expression and tumbled a little further.

"So let me, okay?"

Lost in his indigo gaze, Emma could only nod. They were standing impossibly close. Yet again, he'd merged their space without her realizing it. Barely a breath separated them;

she could feel his body almost touching hers. "You know what else I want?" he asked.

"What?"

The glint behind his smile made her heart race. "Come on. I'll show you."

"I can't believe I let you talk me into a moonlight cruise."

"You can't go to New York and not look at the Statue of Liberty. She is a symbol of freedom, you know."

"At least she's made of stone. I don't think I'm going to feel my toes for days."

"A couple hours soaking in the tub and you'll be fine."

They were in the corridor, in front of Emma's suite. Emma had replaced her shawl with Gideon's jacket, which she'd wrapped tightly around her. Cold feet aside, she'd actually loved the boat ride. There was something incredibly serene about floating on the water, away from the hustle and bustle. Without street noise, the city looked like a picture postcard. She and Gideon had stood at the railing and watched the buildings float silently by. Later, when they turned and Lady Liberty greeted them from the outer harbor,

Gideon had moved behind her, to shield her from the wind. Emma had viewed Staten Island from the shelter of his arms, barely feeling the cold. She was sorry to see the trip end. She was sorry to see the whole night end. Who knew when she'd ever experience another night like this one?

"Thank you," she said, for what had to be the millionth time. "I can't tell you how incredible tonight has been."

"Even with the cold toes?"

She laughed. "Yes, even with the cold toes."

"Good." He reached out and flipped a lock of hair from her shoulder. "And you don't need to keep thanking me. Tonight was my pleasure."

They stood smiling at one another. Emma twisted her key card in her fingers, unsure what to say next. If this had been a date, she could invite him in for a drink.

But this wasn't a date, right? Drinks wouldn't be appropriate.

To play it safe, she returned to her comfort zone. Work. "What time would you like to leave tomorrow?"

Gideon gave her an odd look, one almost

of disappointment. "Back to business, are we, Miss O'Rourke?"

No sense dragging out tonight's fantasy longer than necessary, right? "I don't want to delay you any more than I already have. I know you're eager to head back to Saint Martin. Plus your grandmother's no doubt annoyed you've kept her waiting." As far as Emma knew, he had yet to call with the news about Ross Chamberlain.

"Ah, so you're protecting me from the wrath of Mariah," he teased. "Don't worry, I'll be fine. If not, I can always unleash Hinckley on her again."

"Oooh, that'll teach her," Emma exclaimed. Joking with him was so easy. There were moments, like this one, when she felt like they were on the exact same page.

Perhaps it was a good thing he planned on returning to Saint Martin soon. A woman could easily mistake familiarity for something more. Especially when he smiled the way he was smiling at her.

She cleared her throat. "Well, I should let you go. I know you said to stop, but thank you again for tonight."

"Told you I'd give you a New York experience."

"Yes, you did. For the record, though, I would have settled for the hot dog in the park."

"I know."

While he spoke, she'd started to shrug his jacket off, but he stopped her, reaching out to take the garment by the lapels. She could feel his thumb caress the material. His expression had turned strangely serious. "You're an original, Miss O'Rourke, that's for sure. No fantasies, no need for extravagances, no expectations. Why don't you want more?"

She couldn't. "More" led to disappointment. "I have enough." The thickness in her voice made the words sound hollow.

Fingers brushed her skin as he slipped the jacket from her shoulders. Her breath hitched. When had his hands gotten so warm? They were like fire against her skin.

"Do you?" he asked, his voice low and gravelly. "Because I think you deserve more."

More? "Like what?"

She felt her body leaning toward him, closing the distance between them. She saw his head dip, his eyes grow heavy-lidded.

"Like everything," he whispered.

*Everything.* He made the word sound so possible. Except she didn't need everything. Right now, right here, she didn't need anything.

Then she felt his lips touch her cheek. A gentle lingering kiss that made her knees buckle and her heart stop. Instinctively, she turned toward him, seeking the taste of his mouth. To her disappointment and surprise, he pulled away.

Leaving her wanting more.

"Good night, Miss O'Rourke," he said with a parting caress.

She watched in stunned silence as Gideon disappeared around the corner, while she pressed a shaky hand to where his lips had touched her skin.

# CHAPTER SEVEN

THE NEXT MORNING WAS business as usual. Neither mentioned the night before. They made small talk during the ride to the airport, and the moment they boarded the plane, Gideon barricaded himself with work. "Jamilla, my assistant in Saint Martin, is almost as efficient as you," he teased. "She's managed to fill my in-box in less than twenty-four hours."

Emma smiled, but said nothing. She sat across the aisle, updating her day planner. While part of her appreciated the silence, another part hated that her thoughts had free rein to wander. She knew exactly where they would head, too.

*Don't get carried away.* How often had she thought those words when her mother met a new potential beau? And yet she'd done the exact same thing last night. Too much champagne and candlelight had made her forget reality. Emma pressed her fingertips to her cheek, recalling the feel of Gideon's mouth, hating the stirring the memory caused in her chest. At least now she understood her mother a little better. She could see how easily a woman could get sucked in by romantic fantasy. Last night she'd felt so indescribably special it had been like flying. If that was how her mother felt, then Emma understood why she continued to chase the dream. The high was incredibly addictive.

Except, as with any addiction, when the high ended, you came crashing down. Like she had this morning when she woke up and became plain old Miss O'Rourke again.

She stole a glance across the aisle. Saddest thing was, even knowing about this morning's crash and burn, she would trade her soul for another night like last night.

"Wouldn't you rather go home?" Gideon asked. "I'm sure Mariah doesn't expect you to come in today."

"I want to check my in-box," Emma replied.

They stood watching the parking garage elevator count down the floors. Gideon had hoped Emma would drop him off at the Fairlane and head home, instead of insisting on coming upstairs. He should have known better.

Hopefully, Mariah wouldn't insist on meeting too long. He needed some space to clear his head. Maybe a sail. The brisk air might help. Last night played like a video loop in his head, with every taste, every scent, every touch captured in Technicolor detail. What was he thinking, spouting all that nonsense about her deserving everything? She did, but that wasn't the point. The point was that somewhere between wanting to indulge her, and Ellis Island, he forgot his own rules. He actually started buying all that manufactured romance.

*That's what happens when you spend time with sweet young things,* he told himself. He was beginning to get why all the Kent men continued to make fools of themselves.

Fortunately, his non-Kent genes had kicked just in time, saving him from doing something he'd really regret. Like kissing her senseless and making love to her all night long.

Now if only his body would forget how amazing her skin tasted. He'd had to take a cold shower last night to cool his blood. If a simple peck on the cheek stirred him that much, then her mouth would probably be the death of him. Being stuck in close proximity to her body was bad enough. Every turn, she assaulted him with her doe eyes and vanilla-scented skin. He'd been fighting his body's reaction since LaGuardia.

Maybe he should have gone with the hot dog in the park, after all.

"Should we stop at the front desk and pick up Hinckley's carrier?" Emma asked, all business as usual. She acted as if last night had never happened.

"Hinckley hates the carrier," he replied. "One look and he'll hide. Best I wait till he lets his guard down."

The elevator doors opened and he moved back to let her board. As she passed, vanilla drifted with her. The urge to lean close and inhale gripped him, and he had to struggle not to give in.

By the time he joined her, Emma had already inserted the keycard and stood studying the control panel as if it contained the secrets of the universe. Briefcase in one hand, the other gripping her purse strap, she was an expressionless, efficient, trench-coated statue. Another urge gripped him, this time the desire to grab her shoulders and shake her until she showed some kind of reaction.

Instead he took a position on the other side of the elevator—best he put as much space between them as possible—and checked his watch. "Almost two o'clock. If the elevator doesn't move quickly, I'll have to sit through her soap."

Emma's lips curved slightly, not enough to qualify as a full smile, but enough to make his blood heat. "Maybe she'll make an exception for you."

"Only if hell froze over while we were in the air."

The smile grew a little wider. Gideon wanted more. He wanted a full-blown grin like the ones he'd seen last night.

*Let it go, Gideon. Be grateful she's not calling you out on your behavior.* Last time he checked, kissing your secretary, even if only on the cheek, wasn't exactly proper business behavior.

There was a soft ding, and the elevator doors parted. The small waiting area that served as entrance to Mariah's quarters was empty.

"Odd," Emma said, twisting the door handle. "Your grandmother usually keeps her door unlocked during business hours."

The hair on the back of Gideon's neck prickled. He looked at his watch again. One fifty-nine. "Have you spoken to her today?"

"Earlier, before we took off. We didn't discuss any last-minute appointments." Emma frowned. "Mrs. Kent wouldn't schedule anything for two o'clock, anyway."

"No, she wouldn't," he replied.

He waited impatiently for Emma to unlock the door. Before they could even enter her office, Hinckley was upon them, meowing hoarsely and twisting around their legs. He was the only sign of life.

Emma looked up at Gideon, her face reflecting his worry. "Any reason your grandmother would lock him out?"

"No." His insides turned cold.

The door to Mariah's suite was sealed tight. Their eyes met. Neither of them had to say a word.

*The television set wasn't on.*

"Mariah!" Gideon hollered, banging on

his grandmother's door. "Mariah, are you in there?"

Without waiting for a response, he kicked the door open, knocking the wood panel from its hinges. Emma followed, less than a step behind.

Mariah's sitting room was empty. The television was off. "Mariah!" he called again.

"Gideon?" The faint cry came from the bedroom. In tandem, they ran to the doorway, only to stop short. Gideon's heart sank to the pit of his stomach.

Mariah lay on the floor by the bed, legs tucked awkwardly beneath her. When she saw them, she attempted to sit up, only to wince and fall back again.

He recovered from his shock and rushed to her side. "What happened?"

"I felt dizzy. I went to lie down and I fell. I must have hit—ooh!" She winced again. "My chest. It hurts."

"Shhh, lie still. I'll take care of everything." He stroked her silver hair, hoping he sounded calm, because he sure as hell didn't feel that way.

Emma knelt beside him. "An ambulance is

on the way," she said. "And I asked the front desk to track down your father and uncle."

"Thank you."

"This couldn't have happened too long ago. The bed's made." Meaning the maid had already come and gone. If they hadn't arrived when they did, Mariah might have lain on the floor for God knows how long.

Gideon felt Emma's hand touch his shoulder. It was exactly the reassurance he needed. He gave her a brief, grateful nod and turned his attention back to Mariah. Her pale blue eyes glistened with moisture. Gideon's own vision blurred for a second. All of sudden he was nineteen years old again, his bags packed, listening to Mariah tell him that blood or no blood, he'd always be her grandson. That she would never give up on him.

He stroked the hair from her pale cheek. "Don't worry about anything, Grandmother." Emotion tightened his voice. "I'm here now. I'll take care of everything."

"What's taking so long?" Andrew Kent jammed his fingers through his silver hair before pushing himself from his seat. "We should have heard something by now. Where on earth is Dr. Crenshaw?"

"She said she'd find us as soon as she had some news to share," Gideon replied, in the same firm yet gentle voice he'd been using all afternoon. Jennifer Crenshaw was Mrs. Kent's personal physician. She'd arrived earlier and taken charge of her patient's tests.

Andrew shook his head. "I don't like how long it's taking."

"You can't rush these things. When they do talk to us, I want them to have facts, not speculation, don't you?"

"Gideon's right," Jonathan Kent said softly. "Mother's in good hands. Let Dr. Crenshaw do her job."

Andrew let out a frustrated breath, but didn't argue any further. Like she had in New York, Emma marveled at Gideon's command. He seemed to recognize Andrew's bluster ran in direct proportion to his nerves, and managed his uncle accordingly.

The past couple of hours had been a blur of activity and confusion. Gideon had accompanied his grandmother in the ambulance, while Emma followed behind in the SUV. His father and uncle had arrived at the hospital a short time later. Jonathan Kent looked shell-shocked, while Andrew almost immediately began demanding information, growing frustrated and belligerent when none was forthcoming. That's when Gideon took charge. Watching him calm Andrew down and communicate with the staff, Emma understood immediately why Mrs. Kent wanted him to run Kent Hotels. Calm and collected, even though she knew inside he was as distraught as the others, he was a natural born leader. Her heart swelled with admiration.

Stuck in the middle of the melee, Emma did what she could, getting coffee and retrieving doctor's numbers. But mostly she sat in the corner observing, superfluous to the action around her.

Gideon's father surprised her. Usually charming and loquacious, he sat wordlessly apart from his son, watchful yet distant. Emma might have attributed his aloofness to worry—maybe he was someone who withdrew into himself when faced with adversity—had he not managed to charm the hospital staff, even going so far as to apologize for Andrew's outbursts.

Gideon, she noticed, barely spoke to him,

either. There appeared to be a line drawn between the two that neither wanted to cross.

And yet, as separated from one another as the three men were, they were still an entity unto themselves. A united Kent front, separate and superior.

After what seemed forever, Dr. Crenshaw appeared. She went directly to Gideon. "Your grandmother had a mild heart attack," she told him. "Nothing too severe. More of a wake-up call than anything. She'll need to make some lifestyle changes. The chest pain she complained about was actually from a cracked rib. Apparently she struck the corner of the nightstand when she fell forward."

"So she'll be all right?" Jonathan asked.

Dr. Crenshaw nodded, and all three men's shoulders relaxed with relief. "She'll be up and bossing people around in no time. She's already lecturing the nurses about patient hospitality."

"Heaven help the hospital," Gideon murmured.

"Can we see her now?" Andrew asked.

"Keep it short. I want her to get some rest." Dr. Crenshaw addressed Gideon. "She's asking to see you. When you go in, do me a favor and tell her no hotel business for at least twenty-four hours."

"Like she'll listen to me."

The doctor smiled. "You have as good a chance as anybody."

Gideon disappeared behind Mrs. Kent's hospital door. Emma immediately shivered. With him gone, the corridor felt cold and empty. Andrew and Jonathan turned their backs to her and talked to each other in low tones. They seemed unaware that Emma was even there.

Why *was* she still here? she wondered. For Gideon? He didn't need her. He had his family. She was merely the secretary.

Tossing her empty cup in the trash, she left.

"You gave us quite a scare, missy," Gideon admonished, upon entering his grandmother's room.

"I scared myself," Mariah replied. She looked tiny buried under the covers of her hospital bed. "I hate being helpless."

"Really? I never would have guessed!"

There was a small stool in the corner. He pulled it to the side of the bed and sat down.

The sudden change of height reminded him of younger days and made him smile. "You're going to have to start taking better care of yourself, Mariah."

"I like it better when you use 'Grandmother.'"

So did he. Gideon looked down at the hand resting on his arm. The long tapered fingers were crooked from age, but the touch was a firm as ever. Tightness gripped his chest as he covered those fingers with his own.

"Thank you," she said.

"Shouldn't you be thanking your soap? If you weren't such a creature of habit, we might not have realized something was wrong."

"I'll write the producer a note. I meant thank you for coming home. I've missed you, Gideon."

"I missed you, too." The tightness got a little stronger. This uncharacteristically emotional side of Mariah threatened to dislodge all the feelings he usually kept under control.

He rose to leave. "I better go. Dr. Crenshaw told us not to tire you out, and your sons are pretty eager to check on you."

She squeezed his arm. "Come back tomorrow."

"Of course."

His father and Andrew passed by him on his way out the door. Jonathan looked in his direction for a second, but said nothing. No different than it had been all day, really.

Though there had been one moment. A fleeting instance when, while pacing back and forth, his father had looked in his direction and nodded. As if he was glad Gideon was there with them. And damn if the feeling didn't shake him to the core.

Because he liked it.

A sudden gulf of loneliness opened inside him. Now that the crisis was past, his control slipped and he felt unsteady and adrift. He needed a mooring, an anchorage to steady him.

*Emma.* He needed Emma. From the moment they'd found Mariah, Emma had been there, steady and reassuring. At the peak of the confusion, when Dr. Crenshaw was nowhere to be found and Andrew was bellowing at the nursing staff, Gideon had just had to look at her, sitting quietly next to a rack of linens, to regain his bearings.

He needed some of her steadiness now.

Instinctively, he turned to the chair next to the linen rack.

The chair was empty.


"Emma, open up. It's me."

Emma frowned at her front door, trying to figure out who "me" was. The voice sounded like Gideon Kent's, but that was impossible. He was at the hospital with his family. What's more, he didn't know where she lived.

But it was Gideon. Peering through the peephole, she saw his steely eyes looking back, and a thrill passed through her. Quickly, she quashed her excitement. If Gideon sought her out, it had to be because something was wrong.

She unlatched the door, apparently yanking it open with more force than necessary, for Gideon started. Either that or he was taken aback by her blue plaid flannel pants and pink sweatshirt. Upon coming home from the hospital, she'd been too tired and unsettled to care about matching pajamas. "I woke you up," he said apologetically.

"I was watching television," she assured him. "Is something wrong with Mrs. Kent?"

"Other than being cranky about being laid up, and taking it out on the entire hospital, she's doing all right."

She breathed out in relief. "Good. I'm glad."

On the other hand, something was clearly wrong with Gideon. His cheeks were ruddy, red and windblown, and tension lined his face. He still wore his suit from this morning, though he'd shed the tie and undone the top two buttons of his shirt. The gap revealed a patch of tan, smooth skin.

*Amazing,* thought Emma. Tired and burdened as he looked, he was still devastatingly handsome. She tugged the hem of her sweatshirt in a vain attempt to look fresher. "Would you like some coffee? Tea?"

He shook his head. "I'm caffeined out. Though if you have anything stronger…"

"I don't have whiskey. Will beer do?"

"Beer would be perfect."

"Domestic okay?"

"As long as it contains alcohol, I don't care if you brewed it in your sink."

She headed to the kitchen. Gideon followed, opting to lean against the counter and watch while she fished around in her utensil drawer for a bottle opener. The scrutiny made her suddenly, incredibly sensitive of her surroundings and how far removed they were from the suite at the Landmark, or even his boat. Emma's landlord had spared every expense decorating her side of the duplex. The white laminate cabinets were chipped, and the beige countertops looked as cheap as they probably were. Gideon seemed like a piece of fine art at a flea market in comparison. So why was he here?

"You left the hospital without saying anything," he said.

She was surprised he'd noticed. No one else had. "I didn't want to disturb your visit with your grandmother. Why, did you need something?"

He gave her a long look. "Yes, I did."

"Oh." The hiss of air rushing from the beer bottle filled the kitchen. "I'm sorry. But you said Mrs. Kent was all right, yes?"

"Yes." She handed him his drink, and he took a long sip. "Dr. Crenshaw wants her to stay in the hospital for a night or two."

"I bet she's thrilled about that."

"About as much as you'd expect, but she's

resigned to her fate. I think today frightened her more than she wants to admit."

He took another long drink. Two sips and the bottle was nearly empty. Something *was* off. Gone was the commanding presence from the hospital, replaced by weariness and shadows. "Her accident frightened you, too, didn't it?" Emma murmured.

His response was to drain the last of his bottle. "Got another?"

Yes, this afternoon had definitely shaken him.

"Funny," she said, popping the cap from a second bottle and handing it to him, "but I always think of your grandmother as indestructible."

"She certainly gives that impression. But then, the Kents are very good at false impressions."

What an odd response. He'd said something similar about his father yesterday.

"Nice place you have here," he said, abruptly changing the subject. "Do you live alone?"

She tried hard to pretend his question didn't make her skin tingle. "Yes, why?"

"No reason. Just wondering if I should expect your mother to pop in and join us."

"Good Lord, no. She lives a couple blocks away. We would kill each other if we lived together.

"Besides," Emma added, thinking of the text message she'd received earlier, "she's off on a 'romantic adventure.'" She framed the last two words with her fingers.

"Your mother's got a boyfriend."

"This week, anyway."

That earned her a crooked smile. "Sounds like she took a page from Andrew's book."

"Only without the marriages."

"That could be a good thing. Saves on attorney's fees."

"About all it saves."

"True. They always forget about the collateral damage, don't they?"

A lump stuck in Emma's throat. Talking about her mother only reminded her of last night, and with Gideon standing as close as he was, it was the last thing she wanted to think about. Especially when his voice had that tired, melancholy tone that made her want to comfort him.

Then again, if he had that tone of voice, maybe talking about her mother was a good thing. A verbal cold shower stopping Emma from doing something stupid.

Needing to distract herself from the thickness growing in the room, she grabbed the kitchen sponge and began wiping invisible spills off the Formica. "You said you needed something. What was it?"

"You."

The sponge slipped from her fingers. She gripped the edge of the counter to keep from buckling. "Me?"

"I wanted to thank you. For your help this afternoon."

"Oh." She should have realized. "I only made a few phone calls." He'd been the real unifier.

"You did more than you think."

"Right, I got coffee, too." She gave the counter another unnecessary swipe.

"You were there when we needed you, which means a lot."

How she wished his soft reply didn't make her feel all fuzzy inside. "You could have told me this by phone. I'm sure your family—"

At the word *family,* he gave an irritated snort. "My 'family' will do just fine without me. They have so far."

Not from what Emma had seen at the hospital.

"Funny thing, family," he continued, his voice distant. "What's that old saying, you can pick your friends but—"

"Family's forever."

"I had a different phrase in mind," he said, "but that'll do."

The loneliness behind his words made her heart ache. Was he, she wondered, regretting his estrangement? Or his return?

Meanwhile, Gideon had become intently interested in peeling the label off the bottle neck. The tearing of paper sounded like a foghorn in the silent kitchen.

"Did you know I was raised to run Kent Hotels?" he asked, without looking up.

Emma wasn't surprised, though she was surprised he chose to share the fact with her. "But you don't want to."

"I did once." He raised the bottle to his lips. "But things change, right? Life doesn't always turn out how we plan."

"Seldom does," Emma replied.

"And yet people like Mariah keep fighting to the bitter end. You'd think she'd realize that some things even an iron maiden can't fix."

With one final swig, he emptied the bottle and slapped it on the counter.

"I'm tired," he said abruptly.

"I'm not surprised. Days like today are draining. Especially when the person hurt is someone you care about."

Gideon's eyes met hers. Despite the bright overhead lights, the blue was so dark she couldn't tell where pupil ended and iris began. They were eyes full of despair. "I wish I didn't," he replied, his voice tight.

"Didn't what? Care?" She couldn't imagine that was what he meant.

But it was, because he nodded, and in that one simple gesture, Emma saw all the vulnerability and loneliness he kept tamped down. Her heart swelled, not with pity, but with an emotion far deeper. One she didn't want to contemplate. She simply wanted to offer comfort. To somehow let him know he needn't feel alone.

With a boldness she didn't realize she had, she raised her palm to his face. She didn't say a word. She let her touch do the talking.

The air around them ignited. Suddenly the loneliness in Gideon's eyes disappeared, replaced by something far hotter and primal.

Seeing it, Emma's own desire sprang to life. She traced her fingers down his cheek, letting the stubble burn the tips. Gideon's gaze dropped to her mouth. Anticipation ripped through her body. Her breathing grew ragged. Her lungs couldn't get enough air.

"Emma," he whispered hoarsely.

It was all he said before sweeping her into his arms.

# CHAPTER EIGHT

THERE WAS NO tentativeness, no slow build. Gideon held her tight, his mouth slanting across hers with a passion that, if Emma could breathe, would have taken her breath away.

Her body responded without hesitation. Clinging to the lapels of his coat, she pressed her length to his. Common sense fell away. He needed her. And she wanted him. Wanted *this* more than she'd ever wanted anything in her life.

"Emma, sweet, sweet Emma." Gideon chanted her name between kisses. Hearing him say her first name sounded strange, but incredibly right. His hands slipped under the hem of her sweatshirt and skimmed the hollow above the waistband of her pajama bottoms. Emma let out a sigh. She knew this touch. It was the touch from her dream.

With a soft whimper, she arched closer,

while her hands wrestled Gideon's coat from his shoulders. Who cared if tonight had no future, or that in the morning she'd have to deal with reality? Tonight nothing mattered but this.

Propping himself on one elbow, Gideon stared down at the woman sleeping beside him. She lay curled on her side, lips parted. A strand of hair curled across the bridge of her nose. He smoothed his hand across her forehead, brushing the strand away, and she sighed a sweet sigh.

When he'd left the hospital, he'd only thought to find Emma to talk. He'd called the hotel and cajoled the night manager into looking up her home address, and then he walked here, hoping the combination of brisk night air and Emma's calming presence would rid his head of thoughts he couldn't put words to. Making love had been the last thing on his mind.

Hadn't it?

*Stop kidding yourself.* He knew when Emma answered the door in all her disheveled innocence that this visit couldn't end at simply talking. Being with her was…

He couldn't match words to his thoughts. Only that when she looked at him with those luminous brown eyes, he felt… Why couldn't he think of the right words? *Understood? No longer alone?*

All he knew was the sensation filled his body. He'd reached for her because he couldn't *not* reach for her. He'd needed to feel her, to have her sweet warm presence surround him. She touched something deep inside him in a way that was thrilling and disturbing at the same time.

Emma stirred and pressed closer, her legs entwined with his in unconscious possession. A satisfied smile played on her lips. *He'd caused that smile*. Male pride swelled even as guilt assailed him.

*What happens next?* Mind-blowing night together or not, he was venturing into dangerous territory by sleeping with Emma. She wasn't the kind of woman a man tossed aside after one time, and while he was pretty sure she understood his views on commitment, he didn't want to see her hurt.

Next to him, there was more stirring, and he heard a soft voice say, "Penny for your thoughts?"

Emma's doe eyes were shy and uncertain. Instantly, Gideon's chest constricted. "I was thinking how beautiful you look when you sleep," he answered truthfully. "Like an angel."

Color flushed her skin, reminding him how, only a short time before, she'd flushed with passion. He brushed an imaginary strand of hair from her face, pleased when she shuddered. He wanted her again with a fierceness that shocked him.

"You were smiling," he said. "Good dream?"

"Mmmm." Eyes closing, she burrowed her head in the curve of his neck. "The best."

He wanted her again, more urgently than the first time, if that was even possible. Emma nestled closer, her breath warm on his skin. It was like someone flicked a switch in his body, into the On position. Even the caress of her breathing aroused him.

This was more than dangerous. If he was smart, he'd get up and get out before he dug himself in any deeper.

Only being smart wasn't what he wanted right now.

He gave his sleeping beauty a little nudge. "Hey, don't slip too far into dreamland."

To his surprise, she stiffened and inched off his body. "Sorry, I didn't mean to…."

Was that disappointment in her eyes? The emotion disappeared too quickly for him to tell. That and the fact that Emma had rolled over, putting her back to him. "Have you seen my sweatshirt?" she asked.

"In the kitchen," he replied, snaking his arm around her waist. Surely she wasn't getting dressed? "You don't need to cover up on my account," he teased.

"I'm not. I'm cold, that's all."

Well, he knew how to remedy that situation. Only to his dismay, Emma was slipping from beneath the covers and covering her gloriously naked body with a chenille throw.

"Where are you going?" he asked, pushing himself into a sitting position.

"To get my robe. It's on the hook in the bathroom." She had the throw pulled so tight he wondered how she could breathe.

"Why?"

"I told you, I'm cold."

"I meant why are you getting up at all?" He was beginning to sound like her, asking why, but he didn't couldn't help himself. Since rolling over, she'd yet to look directly at him, which made him a little bit nervous.

"It would be rude to lie in bed while you let yourself out, wouldn't it?"

"Let myself…?"

"Of course. I didn't expect you to stay."

*Why not?* "I wasn't planning on—"

"It's okay. You don't owe me any explanations."

*He didn't?*

"It's been a stressful day. You needed a port in a storm and I—I wanted to give you one."

Finally, she looked at him, though in the dimly lit room he couldn't tell if her expression matched her casual tone. If only he'd thought to turn on more lights when they'd stumbled in here.

"You were more than a port in a storm, Emma" he said.

"Figure of speech." She flashed him what looked like a tremulous smile. "I only mean I know how these things work."

His stomach tensed. What should have given him reassurance for some reason made him more uneasy. "You do?"

"I'm a big girl, Gideon. I knew exactly what I was doing, and the repercussions. So don't worry, I don't expect anything. Now, will you give me a minute? I don't want to walk you to the door naked."

She closed the bathroom door. A few seconds later, Gideon heard the sound of water running.

He sank back, his skull whacking the headboard. *What just happened?*

*Congratulations, Emma, you handled that pretty darn well.*

Eyes burning, she blinked at her reflection in the bathroom mirror, barely recognizing the face blinking back. Tousled hair, swollen lips. She was looking at the face of a sexually satisfied woman. When it came to lovemaking, Gideon was, as always, a man in command of his environment.

It had been glorious.

*Don't get carried away,* she quickly reminded herself. Gideon had been looking for comfort after a stressful day, nothing more. She'd known that when she'd returned his overtures. She wasn't going to compound the situation by expecting more. Nor would she embarrass herself by clinging. She would handle this with sophistication and maturity. She wouldn't think about Gideon's touch or how it made her feel like the most desirable woman in the world. She wouldn't let her lover's prowess cloud reality.

Why, then, did her heart feel as if it was ripping in two?

Drying her face, she slipped on her robe, cringing when she saw the coffee stain on the front, then kicked herself for cringing. A little late to worry about impressions now, wasn't it? She twisted her mussed hair into an even more mussed topknot and opened the door.

Gideon was buttoning his shirt when she walked out. Avoiding his eyes, she crossed the room to her bureau, saying in as casual voice as she could muster, "If you give me a moment, I'll drive you to the marina."

"No need."

"I don't mind. It's late. You'll never catch a cab at this hour." And there was no way he would spend the night. Making small talk over breakfast would be unbearable.

What did one wear when driving home a one-night stand, anyway? She rummaged through the drawer, angry that it mattered to her. She'd finally settled on a beige sweater when a hand came down on her forearm, halting her search.

Apology lined Gideon's face. "Don't."

Her knees faltered, along with her veil of sophistication. She floundered for footing, desperately thinking of something neutral to say in response. "Feels like it's getting colder. I wouldn't be surprised if we have snow flurries. But then that's New England for you, right? Snow in October."

He opened his mouth to reply. She cut him off.

"It's all right, Gideon. I already told you I understood." And she wasn't up to rehashing. "You don't owe me any explanations." Or apologies. *Please, no apologies.* "Now let me get dressed so I can take you to your boat."

"Don't get dressed," he said. "I'll walk. It's not that far."

"Oh. Sure." He wasn't apologizing, after all; he was just eager to escape her company. How embarrassing. She furiously blinked back the tears springing to her eyes.

Wordlessly, they headed to where the night had begun—her kitchen. His coat lay in a heap on the floor, the sleeve draped over her discarded sweatshirt, an intimate reminder of what had transpired. Emma looked away. The awkwardness in the room was growing exponentially. No wonder Gideon wanted out quickly.

"Can I get you some coffee? For the road," she added, in case he thought her offer a ploy for him to stay. "I've got travel mugs."

"I think I've had enough to drink, coffee and otherwise."

Yes, she thought, casting a glance at the empty beer bottles, maybe he had.

Too bad she didn't have the same excuse.

She waited while he shrugged into his jacket, then led him to the front door. To her relief Gideon didn't try to draw her into conversation. That is, until she touched the door handle. Then he reached out and covered her hand. "I don't want—"

"Gideon, I'm fine," she said, determinedly bright. Other than wanting to melt back against him as soon as he touched her, that is. "Tell your grandmother I'll be by first thing tomorrow morning. If you'd like, I can call first. To make sure I don't interrupt any tests." Along with giving them a chance to avoid each other.

An unreadable emotion flickered across Gideon's face as he brushed a strand of hair from her temple. The tenderness nearly killed her, and she had to brace herself against the door to withstand the impact.

His fingers trailed downward, along her cheekbone, until they curled around her jaw, drawing her forward. Her traitorous body began to hum. It took every ounce of her resolve to turn her head at the last second.

Didn't matter. He found her lips, anyway. "Good night, Emma," he whispered.

She mustered a smile. "Goodbye, Gideon."

"Another arrangement? Good grief, don't these people have something better to do with their money?"

Emma wondered the same thing. Mrs. Kent's hospital room resembled a florist's shop. Three deliveries arrived during her visit alone. Large, expansive arrangements from Boston's top florists. They dwarfed the small get-well bouquet she'd purchased at the hospital gift shop, and filled the air with thick fragrance.

She'd so had enough of flowers today.

Before visiting the hospital, she'd stopped

by the hotel, where the concierge told her a dozen red roses were waiting. At first she'd thought they were for Mrs. Kent, until she noticed the card addressed to her. Gideon had sent them. Roses, apparently, were the obligatory custom following a one-night stand. She'd left them in the box, hoping out of sight would equal out of mind. But all these flowers were quickly proving that theory wrong. Maybe she should bring Gideon's bouquet here. Let them blend in with the others.

"They're from the governor." She read the card stuck amid the blooms. "He wishes you a speedy recovery." Gideon's card had only his name. Could've been worse, she realized. He could have added some lame closing, such as "Fondly."

She looked around the room. "Where would you like me to put it? Space is at a premium."

"Send the foolish thing to the nurse's station. As a matter of fact, send all the plants there," Mrs. Kent replied. "I can't take the smell."

Emma couldn't blame her. All the flowery scents were giving her a headache. "Unfortunately, I doubt this is the last. If you'd like, I can arrange for the flowers to go to other patients. Maybe the geriatric ward?"

"What a wonderful idea. Let them brighten up someone else's room. Take an arrangement for your desk, too," Mariah added. "You look like you could use some brightening."

So much for the concealing powers of makeup. After Gideon left last night, Emma had spent an hour or two curled on the sofa, mentally kicking herself. Then, because she couldn't bear the idea of sleeping on sheets that bore his scent, she'd spent the rest of the night doing laundry. As a result, she looked like the walking dead, pinched and drawn in her jeans and dark sweater.

"I'm fine," she lied. "Just tired after yesterday. You gave everyone quite a scare."

"So my sons keep reminding me. They're making a far bigger fuss than necessary, if you ask me."

Her protest might have carried more weight if she hadn't attempted to sit straighter while speaking, and gasped in pain.

"They're concerned about you," Emma replied. "Do you want the bed raised?"

"What I want is to go home to my own bed," Mrs. Kent grumbled. At that moment she resembled a petulant child rather than the matriarch of a billion-dollar empire.

To hide her smile, Emma grabbed the plastic water jug next to the bed and topped off her employer's ice water. "Dr. Crenshaw's also concerned."

"Dr. Crenshaw is a middle-aged worry-wart."

"Dear God, this place looks like the inside of a florist's."

Gideon's voice sounded from the doorway, causing Emma to jerk her hand back and send water sloshing over the nightstand. For once she was grateful for her clumsiness, because she could avoid looking up. She grabbed a handful of tissues and tried not to think about the man whose footsteps were entering the room.

To her chagrin, the footsteps rounded the bed and stopped behind her.

"Sorry I startled you," he murmured. His breath was warm against the back of her neck, reminding her of last night, when that same breath had been hot and steady on her skin. Just like last night, Emma's insides began to tremble.

"Good morning," she heard him say to

Mariah, followed by a soft noise that sounded like a kiss on the cheek.

"I see you decided to look your best for this visit," Mrs. Kent said in greeting.

"And I see you're feeling better. How did this morning's tests go?"

"Humph, tests. Dr. Crenshaw's a little too fond of tests. If you ask me, she's using them as an excuse to run up my bill."

"Really? I thought you said she was a middle-aged worrywart." Emma could hear the smile in Gideon's voice. "Wasn't that the phrase she used, Miss O'Rourke?"

Emma kept her eyes on the table in front of her. "I believe so, Mr. Kent."

"Nice to know you two are keeping records of everything I say. I thought you were coming by earlier."

"I stopped by the hotel to pick up Hinckley before he took over your bedroom."

"Too late. That three-legged monster made himself quite at home on the first night. On my cashmere throw, no less."

"That's Hinckley. Nothing but the best. Right, Miss O'Rourke?"

Why couldn't he ignore her presence and talk to his grandmother? Reluctantly, she looked up. *Please don't let there be indifference in his eyes,* she prayed. That would be worse than the flowers.

She should have prayed for something else. Like her legs not turning to jelly, or for Gideon not to look quite so perfect.

No wonder Mrs. Kent had made a comment about his clothes. He'd reverted back to sailor mode—faded jeans and that ratty Irish-knit sweater—and looked as beautiful and awe-inspiring as ever. Emma's heart gave a sad little lurch.

"I'll send the throw out to be dry-cleaned," she said.

"Never mind." Mrs. Kent waved away the comment. "Gideon might as well take it with him, since that creature is so fond of the thing."

"Ah, but then he won't want to sleep on it anymore," Gideon told her. "Where's the fun in sleeping on something you're *allowed* to sleep on?"

*Or with,* thought Emma bitterly.

"Sorry to interrupt," a nurse said, knocking on the door, "but it's time to check Mrs. Kent's vital signs." Her eyes swept over Gideon with obvious attraction as she approached the bed.

Gideon smiled back, causing Emma's stomach to knot with jealousy.

*Knock it off,* she told herself sternly. *You don't have any claim on him.*

Meanwhile, the nurse practically beamed, she smiled so brightly. "If you'd like to wait, I promise I won't take long."

Seeing her chance to escape, Emma scooped the flowers from Mrs. Kent's bedside table. "I'm going to take this to the nurse's station and make those arrangements we talked about." After which she'd slip into the elevator, and finish visiting later, after Gideon left.

Or not.

Ten steps from the room, she heard Gideon call out, "Emma, wait!"

Her heart urged her to pretend she didn't hear. Unfortunately, her brain told her that wouldn't work, so she stopped.

"Apparently the nurse watches *All My Loves,*" he said, catching up. "At least I hope so. They're in there discussing who fathered some woman's baby."

"The ex-husband," Emma replied automatically.

"How do you know?"

"It's always the ex-husband."

"You'd think I'd know that by now." Without asking, he took the floral arrangement from her. "So Mariah's giving flowers to the nurses?"

"Among others." She told him the plan to deliver flowers to other patients.

"Nice idea. Yours?"

Hating how his compliment made her insides turn mushy, she focused on the flecks embedded in the gray linoleum. "Your grandmother wanted to spread the wealth."

"Just don't give away all the flowers that get delivered."

She paused, then realized what he meant. "The roses."

"Good, you got them. I was going to send them to your place, but didn't want them sitting on your doorstep all day." His mouth quirked. "For some reason I figured I'd have better luck sending them to you at work."

"They're lovely," she replied quietly.

"Not nearly as lovely as the recipient, I assure you."

Again, her insides melted. "You don't have to do that, you know."

"What, send flowers? I wanted to."

"I mean the compliments. There's no need to let me down easy. I told you last night I didn't expect anything."

He regarded her for a long moment. "Most women would."

"Guess I'm more realistic than most."

They reached the nurse's station, where the head nurse was on the phone, updating someone on a patient's condition. When she saw them approach, she signaled that she'd be another minute.

Gideon set the flowers on the counter. "Do you really think I'm trying to let you down easy?"

"Aren't you?"

"Funny, I thought I was showing my admiration."

The nurse on the phone signaled that she'd be a few more moments. Emma busied herself with the arrangement, repositioning chrysanthemums.

Gideon's voice came from behind her shoulder. "What are you doing tonight?"

"Tonight?"

"Yes, it follows this afternoon."

"Why?"

"Because I thought we could have dinner on my boat," he replied.

"That's not necessary."

"Why don't you let me be the judge of that?"

She adjusted another stem. From the corner of her eye, she saw the nurse wrapping up her phone conversation. Or so Emma hoped. She needed the interruption. Gideon's question gave birth to an optimism she didn't want to feel. He was only inviting her out of guilt, trying to make amends for last night. Like with the roses.

"I have to make arrangements for the flowers," she said.

"You haven't accepted my invitation yet." He lowered his head towards her. To the nurses at the station, it would look as if he was merely speaking confidentially. Except that he used the same maddening lover's voice he'd used in her bed. The one that coaxed her to do whatever he wanted. "You know you want to."

Heaven help her, but she did. She wanted another night with his hands on her skin and his voice murmuring lover's words in her ear. What good would it do, though, except to pull her back into the orbit of a man she was better off forgetting?

Gideon's fingers curled around her shoulders. "I'm waiting."

The fissure dividing common sense and want widened. This whatever-they-were-doing had no future, no point. Only a glutton for punishment would say yes.

She sighed. "What time?"

Was she making a mistake? Probably, but making a mistake apparently didn't stop her from finding her way to the marina at sundown.

Gideon's hatchway was open. Light and the aroma of Italian food spilled out into the cockpit. He'd told her to dress warmly and she had, in jeans and a wine-colored sweater she knew set off her hair. Even so, a shiver ran through her as she stepped aboard. *What are you doing?* she asked herself yet again. Another night would only make the inevitable that much harder.

Suddenly changing her mind, she turned to leave, but before she could run, Gideon's head appeared in the hatchway opening. "I thought I heard footsteps," he called. "Come on down."

Emma found she couldn't say no. With tentative steps, she headed toward him.

The cabin looked different than the last time she'd seen it. For one thing, the brass lamps were dimmed to their lowest setting. As their gimbals swayed with the current, they flickered like candles. The table was set for two with fine china and silver. With slight amusement she recognized the pattern as the same one from the Fairlane dining room. A vase with a single rose graced the middle. An open bottle of wine waited next to two crystal goblets.

It reminded her of New York.

Gideon never looked better. He'd shaved, and ditched the sweater in favor of a white shirt that pulled tight across his chest. Dark curls teased the open neck. He was gazing at her like he'd never seen a woman before. The unabashed desire stirred hers.

"You wore your hair down," he drawled. "I like it."

"Thank you."

He moved forward, eyes locked on her. Emma's mouth went dry. She regretted wearing such a heavy sweater, because she was suddenly quite hot. Another couple steps and there'd be no space between them.

"I'm looking forward to dinner," she said.

"Me, too."

He came closer. Emma started to tremble with need. "I'm hungry," she managed to say.

"Me, too."

He reached the stairs, then reached for her. Emma's vision glazed as she melted into his embrace. Immediately his fingers tangled in her hair, urging her mouth to his. "Let's start with dessert."

# CHAPTER NINE

"I'M REARRANGING DECK furniture, aren't I?"

Hinckley blinked at her. At the moment he lay sprawled across the seat cushion, far more interested in having his fur stroked than listening to her ramble.

It had been three days since Mrs. Kent's heart attack. Three nights with Gideon. Here, on morning four, Emma found herself repeating the same argument as days one through three—that being with Gideon was a bad idea with a capital B.

"Our ship's going nowhere but down," she told Hinckley. "I should get off before I drown, right?"

Except she wasn't entirely sure she wasn't over her head already.

She stared at the red streaks painting the horizon. Gideon was below, sleeping. Or so she presumed, from the soft snoring she'd heard as she slipped from the sheets about an hour before. As had become her habit these last couple of days, she'd gone on deck to watch the sunrise. This morning the October wind blew wet with the remnants of last night's fog. Shivering, she pulled the sweatshirt hood over her head, only to shiver again because the thick cotton smelled like Gideon. She inhaled deeply, savoring the aroma like a women in a fabric softener commercial. Maybe he'd let her keep the shirt when he left.

*When he left*. Her heart sank a little. As much as she tried to live in the moment, thoughts of his inevitable departure dogged her, anyway.

Bringing her back to the deck chairs.

Hinckley nudged her thigh, demanding attention. "Yeah, I know, stop talking and put my fingers to better use," she replied, finding the sweet spot between his two shoulder blades. The action flipped a switch, and the feline immediately rolled onto his back, his three limbs stretching straight in the air so she could scratch his belly. The purr in his throat rivaled the fishing boats' engines.

"If only we could all be more like you," she told him.

"Please, the world couldn't handle that much self-centeredness."

Gideon emerged from the hatchway, two cups of coffee in his hands. His smile flipped Emma's switch, and her heart sped up. Lord, but he was handsome in the morning. He was handsome any hour of the day, but mornings, when his eyes were the bluest part of the world, were especially good to him. Today he'd showered before coming up. His damp hair had a little bit of curl in the back.

"I thought I'd find you up here," he said, handing her a cup. "You're turning into quite the sea dog, you know that?"

She breathed in the steam wafting from her mug. "I never knew how pretty the harbor could be this time of the morning. The solitude's very peaceful."

"That it is." Settling on the other side of Hinckley, he gave the cat's jaw a scratch. Which of course Hinckley responded to by stretching and making room for more hands on his body.

Gideon chucked. "Reminds me of someone

else I know," he teased. "Must be my magic hands."

Emma stuck out her tongue. He didn't need the encouragement, even if he was right. "More likely it's having two sets of hands on him at once."

"True. Heaven help him when he has to go back to one-person attention."

Meaning when Gideon left Boston. They hadn't talked about his leaving, but with Mrs. Kent out of the hospital, the time was coming. A lump rose in Emma's throat. To ignore it, she studied the trails their fingers made in Hinckley's fur. "I'm sure he'll adjust. Cats always do." Same as she would.

"I don't know. He's pretty spoiled."

"I think he's proved he can roll with life's punches, don't you?"

"Maybe, but you can roll only so many times."

It didn't feel like they were discussing Hinckley anymore.

The sun had breached the horizon and was painting the gray with pink streaks. She pointed toward the light. "Red sun at dawn, sailor's forewarned, right?"

"Listen to you quoting seamen's myths.

Next thing you know you'll be singing sea shanties and munching hardtack."

"Don't forget the parrot on my shoulder."

"A parrot, huh?"

"A girl's got to assimilate."

"And you assimilate so adorably, too." He leaned over and kissed the tip of her nose.

This was how they worked. Deliberately steering the conversation to lighter fare, sharing but not sharing. As if they both knew delving too deeply would be a mistake.

Indignant that their teasing interrupted his massage, Hinckley stretched and got off the bench. Gideon used the opportunity to scoot closer to Emma. She leaned back against his chest, and together they watched the sun rise higher.

"Tell me," he said after a few moments, his chin coming to rest on her shoulder, "does this new assimilation of yours mean you're planning to accept my offer?"

Sailing lessons. Last night he'd offered to teach her.

Emma shook her head. "I think I'll draw the line at forecasting. I told you last night, the ocean's a bit too cold for me at the moment."

"And I told you, you could come to Saint Martin. *Mi casa es su casa.*"

"I thought they spoke French on your part of the island."

"Okay, *ma maison est votre maison*. Or should I say *mon bateau est votre bateau?*"

*My boat is your boat.* She couldn't think of anything more enticing than being with Gideon on a tropical island, but they both knew the invitation wasn't serious. "Thanks, but I think we're all better off if I stay on dry land."

"You navigated the water all right last night."

Color crept into her cheeks as she remembered how they'd made love to the rhythm of the waves. "That was different. The boat wasn't actually moving."

"Says you."

He caught her chin, reeling her in for a quick kiss. His touch was so warm and gentle, and felt so good that Emma was surprised she didn't start purring like Hinckley. "You'd make a helluva first mate," he said against her lips.

When he dropped his voice like that it was hard to remember this was only banter. Emma bit back a sigh. Her index finger traced his lower lip before trailing to his collar. He wore a white button-down shirt. "You're dressed for business," she mused.

"Breakfast summit," he explained. "Mariah issued an edict for first thing this morning."

"That's right. I forgot." Arranging the breakfast had been one of Emma's first tasks when Mrs. Kent came home.

She took a long, fortifying sip of coffee. "I better head to the shower."

She moved to get up, but he caught her wrist. "Whoa, no need for you to rush."

"Are you kidding? When your grandmother says first thing, she means first thing."

"For her sons and me. For you, on the other hand, there's absolutely no reason to rush. She'll have you doing her bidding all day. Take your time, have a second cup of coffee, pleasure Hinckley. Better yet, think about ways I can pleasure you later."

With that, he leaned forward and kissed her. She expected he meant the kiss to be a quick peck, but as usual, what started innocently enough quickly ignited into something more, erasing all coherent thought. Emma sighed into Gideon's mouth as he pulled her tight.

He tasted of coffee and spearmint and something more. Something unmistakably Gideon. It was incredible, and totally, completely addictive. She was putty in his hands.

"Emma," he whispered, when they finally broke apart. He pressed his forehead to hers, his ragged breathing matching hers. "I so don't want to go to breakfast."

She so didn't want him to go. "But your grandmother…"

"I know." He broke away, but not before emitting a guttural groan. "We'll continue this tonight, okay?"

Emma nodded. She couldn't have refused if she wanted to.


When did his uncle become such a pompous ass?

Gideon sat back in his seat, listening as the man described, of all things, coffee grind and eggshell facial wraps. Had to be Suzanne's influence. The man was working overtime to make this marriage stick. Good luck with that.

Gideon tried to picture Emma having a coffee grind facial, and failed. No matter. He'd much rather picture her as she'd been this morning, anyway. Hands and head tucked in his sweatshirt, with only her face visible to the morning. Well, her face and her legs. Those long, long legs. He shifted uncomfortably and wished for the umpteenth time he had stayed with Emma on the boat. From the disappointment he'd caught in her eyes when he'd disembarked, she did, too.

Funny, he'd thought he would have gotten her out of his system by now, but the opposite held true. If anything, the past three days had whetted his appetite for more. And given Emma's uninhibited response to his lovemaking, he had to assume she was as hungry for more as he was.

Why didn't she want to go to Saint Martin, then? They were having a good time together. Why not extend the fun a little longer under the hot tropical sun? He could show her all the sights he'd described to her. Those places that made her eyes light up with fascination. Maybe they could jet over to Cabo. He could picture her face now as she watched the sunset. Eyes growing wide, lips parting in a small O, the way they did just before she—

"Gideon?"

"Hmm?" He jerked his attention back to Mariah.

"I asked if Ross had anything else to say when you met with him," she stated.

"Nothing I haven't already told you. He seemed satisfied that Kent Hotels had a solid future. Why?"

"Because I got a message yesterday from Gerard Ambiteau. He was inquiring about my health."

"You did have a heart attack, Mother," Andrew said. "He's simply showing professional courtesy."

"Nonsense. Gerard Ambiteau doesn't believe in courtesy. He smells blood in the water. That's why we need to make sure we have Ross Chamberlain's loyalty. Thank goodness I didn't have my heart attack twenty-fours earlier."

"Mother!"

"I'm simply pointing out a fact." Mariah set down her tea. "We dodged a big bullet the other day. There's no guarantee that next time we'll be so lucky."

Gideon sipped his orange juice, which had suddenly lost its flavor. He didn't want to talk about a next time, with regards to business or Mariah's health. Both topics churned his stomach and made his heart burn. It didn't help that Jonathan sat through the entire meeting like some kind of stone statue, barely saying a word. If not for the occasional sidelong glance, one would think Jonathan didn't know his supposed firstborn was even in the room.

Using his glass as a screen, Gideon stole a look to his left. Jonathan was intent on his egg-white omelet and didn't look up. Gideon's heartburn kicked up a notch. From the hollow sensation beneath his rib cage, he was pretty sure the acid had burned a hole in his chest.

As soon as this breakfast ended, he was taking Emma for a long solitary walk and some fresh air.

"And then there's our other shareholders," Mariah continued. "What about them?"

"Most of them are family," Andrew noted.

"Being family doesn't equate loyalty. The way this family's gone to hell in a handbasket the past few years, I wouldn't be surprised if they lined up to sell us out. Unless they feel Kent Hotels is in good hands."

"And how do we convince them of that?" Andrew asked.

Mariah looked unwaveringly at Gideon and raised her teacup to her lips. "Simple," she stated. "We name a successor."

"Gideon, wait!"

Emma was returning from the business center when she heard Jonathan call his son's name. His tone, unsure and soft, stopped her in her tracks. She hovered outside her office door, uncertain what to do.

"Yes?" she heard Gideon say.

"I—We—never thanked you for everything you did the other day. With your grandmother. Keeping Andrew under control."

"You don't need to thank me. I was simply doing what needed to be done." He sounded like her, Emma thought with a smile. She'd have to tease him later.

"Yes, we do," the elder Kent insisted. "If you hadn't arrived when you did…" Silence filled the air. Unable to help herself, Emma peered through the door crack. Gideon and his father stood face-to-face, much closer together than she would have guessed from their stilted voices. Jonathan Kent was looking down, toeing the carpet with his Italian loafer. "Your grandmother didn't tell me you were coming to Boston." He looked up with a nervous smile. "I think she feared I would bolt."

"I'm surprised you didn't," Emma heard Gideon say under his breath.

"Guess I deserved that. It's been a long time."

"Ten years."

"You've done well for yourself."

"You paid attention?"

"Of course." Jonathan's expression was one of forlorn surprise. A mirror, Emma suspected, of Gideon's face seconds before. "Why wouldn't I?"

"Because it's been ten years."

Emma knew she should back away. This was a intimate moment between father and son, one she had no business watching. But she couldn't move. Gideon stood with posture so erect and proud it broke her heart.

Again, Jonathan toed the carpet. "I suppose you'll be heading back soon, to Saint Martin."

"Well, there isn't any real reason for me to stay, is there?" Emma's heart crumbled when she heard Gideon's answer.

"There's your grandmother's offer. I thought perhaps you might reconsider. The family…" Jonathan cleared his throat. "Your family needs you."

"*My* family?" Gideon responded with cynicism.

"Yes, your family. We need you." Jonathan touched Gideon's shoulder. "I know what you're thinking, but no matter what, your last name is and always will be Kent. That makes this your family. It makes you *my* family."

There was no response. Emma saw Gideon bow his head. Jonathan kept his hand on his son's shoulder. "I should have told you that a long time ago. But then you left, and I kept waiting for the right time, and…" He gave a halfhearted shrug. "The more time that passed, the less sure I was you'd listen."

"Why?" Gideon's voice cracked, as if he was choking on the words. Emma's heart cracked with it. "Why now?"

"In a word? Mother. Her heart attack made me realize that if I kept dragging my feet, I might run out of time altogether. Then I'd never get to tell you at all."

More silence. Gideon was weighing his father's words. "Are you sure this has nothing to do with Mariah's offer?" he asked after a moment.

"Perhaps a little. You should be where your heart is, Gideon."

"And you think my heart's in Boston?" His disdain was palpable. Emma felt the stab.

"I think only you can answer that question. But why else would you come back?"

"Because Mariah asked me to."

"And you've stayed…"

Again, no response.

Jonathan started toward the elevator. Emma ducked around the corner so Gideon wouldn't catch her eavesdropping. She'd just made it when his voice called out.

"Jon—Dad, wait." He caught up with his father. "I'm going to be here a couple more days. Would you like to have a cup of coffee… or something?"

Gratitude lit Jonathan's expression in a way Emma had never seen before. "I'd like that. Are you free now?"

"Yeah," Gideon replied in a hoarse whisper. "I'm free now."

The elevator cane and went, leaving Emma alone. She stayed hidden around the corner, not yet ready to leave her coward's hideout.

*Nothing to keep me here. You think my heart's in Boston?*

Talk about a wake-up call. More like an air siren blasting in her ear.

It wasn't as if she hadn't expected that. Hadn't she been saying pretty much the same thing to Hinckley this morning? At least now she knew when her ship would sail: in a couple days.

A couple more days, then back to reality.

Reality came sooner than she thought. It arrived about eight hours later, when her mother turned up at her apartment in tears over her latest heartbreak.

"Tony and I had a connection, you know?" she said between sniffles. "We had a bond."

"I know, Mom." There was always a connection.

Janet had wedged herself into the corner of Emma's couch. Her knees were pulled tight to her chest, and she was taking shaky drags on a cigarette. An ashtray filled with cigarette remains rested by the sofa arm. Mascara streaked her cheeks. It was the only makeup she still had on, the rest having been cried or worn off.

"He was so nice," she continued, before pausing for another puff. "Did I mention he had a boat? And a house on the Vineyard? We talked about me visiting, for cripe's sake."

She ground the butt in the ashtray, grabbed her pack and lit another. "What did I do wrong?"

"Nothing, Mom." *You just read too much into the conversation*. As usual. "He's a jerk, that's all."

"But I really, really liked him."

She always did. And as she got older, she fell faster and harder, the endings more bitter and dramatic.

"It's not fair," Janet said. "Why do they always dump me?"

Emma's stomach churned as she handed her mother a fresh tissue. They'd been through the breakup regime dozens of times. No sense suggesting her mother caused her own misery, since she wouldn't listen. Besides, this time Emma actually had a little sympathy for Janet's woe-is-me sobs.

After all, she was heading for same scenario.

*Nothing to keep me here*. She shook off Gideon's words. Now wasn't the time. Her mother would cry her eyes out for at least another couple hours, before falling asleep on the sofa. There would be plenty of time for a pity party then.

As she listened to Janet ramble on about heartache and the inequities of life, Emma wondered how many times the universe would have to crush her mother's romantic dreams before she got the message. Janet's meltdown was just one more reminder that her own affair with Gideon was a one-way cruise to nowhere. She refused to be like the woman in front of her, crying over a love affair that existed only in her mind.

Time to abandon ship.

It was two hours later when she arrived at the marina. When she'd called to cancel their date earlier, Gideon had told her he would welcome her no matter what time she arrived, but now she wondered if she should have waited until morning. The boat looked dark.

Drawing closer, however, she saw a light in the front berth. *Gideon was in bed.* She pictured him propped against the cushions, his chest bare and muscular in the dim light.

Maybe one more night…

No, no more nights. That's how she'd gotten into this mess in the first place. One night would stretch to two and then three, and before she knew it, Gideon would set sail along with whatever chance she had of keeping her dignity intact. No waiting until morning, either. Because come morning, she'd only find another reason to stall. Either she ended things now or she ended them never.

Squaring her shoulders, she stepped aboard and knocked on the hatchway door. Gideon answered within moments. "Emma!" he said in surprise, before his expression softened in what seemed to be genuine pleasure.

He looked exactly as she'd pictured, shirtless and sexy as could be. Emma's heart immediately lodged in her throat. This would be harder than she'd thought.

"Can I come aboard?" she asked.

"Of course. Why didn't you call? I would have picked you up. You shouldn't be wandering around alone this time of night."

"I didn't want to be a bother."

He rolled his eyes. "What will I do with you? Come on," he said, extending a hand, "get inside before you let the cold air out. Is everything all right? You sounded off when you called."

"My mother had a temporary crisis. Nothing I haven't dealt with before."

"You sure? You look tired."

Gentle concern marked his expression. Emma tried desperately not to fall under its spell. Too much tenderness would make her task impossible. "Dealing with my mother can be draining."

"Obviously. Let me get you something to drink."

"You don't have to."

"Will you stop being a martyr?" He gave her shoulders a gentle kneading. "I know I don't *have* to anything," he whispered. The huskiness in his voice went straight to her insides.

*Please stop being so wonderful,* she begged silently.

He disappeared into the galley, leaving her alone. The respite helped her regain her bearings, and she took a long last look at her surroundings. Of all the wonderfully luxurious locations she'd seen since meeting Gideon, the boat would always be her favorite. The jet was incredible, the Landmark was luxurious, the restaurant beyond words, but this space felt…real. Her eyes began to burn.

"Penny for your thoughts."

Why did his voice always manage to send tingles down her spine? "I was thinking about the first time I came on board," she said, blinking her eyes quickly.

"A rain-soaked Little Match Girl." His chest was a breath away from her spine. He slipped an arm around her waist and pulled her close. "I'm glad you didn't freeze to death that day."

"Me, too." She looked down at the mug Gideon had placed in her hands. "Tea?" she noted with surprise.

"I grabbed a box while stocking supplies. Figured you might appreciate having some on board. That is your blend, no?"

"Yes." Her eyes began blurring again. Why was he making this so hard? "Thank you."

If Gideon noticed her strangled tone of voice, he didn't comment. He was too busy nuzzling her neck. "I told you, *mon bateau est votre bateau*. Besides, it's all part of my master plan."

"Master plan?" She was trying not to arch

her neck in response to his kisses, and failing miserably.

"I figure if I stock the boat with your favorite foods, your practical nature will force you to visit me in Saint Martin. Because I know you don't like to waste food."

He trailed kisses up her neck, his tongue flicking the skin under her jaw. Emma squeezed her eyes tight, willing herself not to melt. "I'm not visiting you in Saint Martin." She managed to grind out the words.

"So you say now. I haven't finished implementing the plan yet. Food is only part of the strategy. Care to guess the other part?" he asked as he nipped her earlobe.

"Not really."

Somehow she summoned the strength she needed to break their embrace and move to the other side of the cabin. As distance went, it wasn't much, but it was enough to clear her head. A little.

She could feel Gideon frowning at her back. "What's wrong? I thought you said everything went okay with your mother."

"It did."

"Then why are you so tense? Did something else happen?"

A whole lot had happened, beginning with her waking up. "I'm not going to Saint Martin," she repeated.

"Why not? We both know you'd have a terrific time. You, me, the tropical breezes…"

He closed the distance between them in three short steps, causing Emma to curse the narrowness of sea vessels. If she'd been smart, she'd have insisted on staying outside to talk.

"There's so many things I want to show you," he continued in that lover's voice she'd come to adore. "Places you wouldn't believe exist."

As he spoke, he traced a path with his index finger down the side of her neck and along the curve of her shoulder. Her sweater did nothing to stop the heat of his touch from reaching her skin. "Beautiful, tropical hideaways where no one can find us. What do you say, Emma. Will you let me show you?"

It sounded heavenly. Beyond her wildest dreams. She sighed. Then, just as she felt her defenses begin to crumble, an image of her mother sobbing popped into her head, renewing her resolve.

"Like you showed me New York?" she asked, breaking away. "Another treat for the poor travel-deprived secretary?"

Gideon's evasive expression told her she'd hit upon some truth. Sensing her opportunity, she continued. "That's what this has been all about, hasn't it? Expanding the poor Little Match Girl's world? Giving her some fantastical memories?"

"Since when is it a crime to treat a woman like a princess?" he asked.

Except she wasn't a princes, she was a secretary. "It's not a crime," she replied. "Just very seductive."

"And that's a bad thing?"

He reached for her, but she sidestepped in time. "Yes, it is. Because eventually the experiences have to end, and the pretend princess has to go back to her life. Don't worry, though, I knew exactly what I was getting into when we started this little fling."

A shadow crossed his features, making his expression impossible to read. "Is that what you think we're doing? Having a fling?"

"What else would you call it? You don't do relationships, remember?"

Saying the words out loud hurt more than she expected. Needing a moment to collect herself, she gulped down her tea. The hot liquid burned her throat, but she didn't care. It made her temporarily forget the pain in her chest.

Gideon, of course, said nothing, which spoke volumes.

"Like I said, don't worry," she repeated, as much to reassure herself as to reassure him. "I'm a big girl. I never harbored expectations that what we were doing would lead to anything more."

"You didn't." He sounded as if he didn't believe her. She supposed because he was used to the opposite.

"I learned a long time ago that life isn't a fairy tale, Gideon. Happy endings are few and far between. And I've seen more times than I can count what happens when you base your future on false hope." She forced a tremulous smile. "Better to live in reality then nurse a fantasy. Wouldn't you agree?"

He didn't answer. Trying to think of an appropriate response, no doubt. What, she wondered, did someone say in a situation such as this, other than goodbye? Surely nothing that would make the ending any easier.

And so when Gideon finally did open his mouth to speak, she pressed her fingers to his lips. "Don't. Let's not belabor what we both know is the truth. Why don't we both walk away while we're still friends, happy with the fun we had together?"

He didn't answer. She didn't let him. That didn't stop disappointment from hitting her hard. In spite of everything, part of her wanted him to argue the point, even though they both knew there was no point in doing so. Proof she was right to end things between them.

It was time to go. Her teacup was empty. Setting the mug down, she gave Gideon one last smile, backing away when he reached for her. She wanted nothing more than to taste one last kiss, but she knew doing so would hurt far too much. "I want you to know that this...us—" she waved her hand between them "—was amazing. I don't think I've ever felt... Never mind." She had been about to say special, but the word sounded trite. "Goodbye, Gideon."

He stared, shocked. "You're leaving?"

"We'd both be better off if I did, don't you

think?" She grabbed the railing. "Have a safe journey home, Gideon."

Before he could utter another word, she bolted up the stairs.

# CHAPTER TEN

TOO STUNNED TO SAY A WORD, Gideon watched as Emma raced away. It wasn't until he heard the footsteps above him that he realized what had happened, and sprang into action.

"Emma, wait!"

He bounded up on deck. "Emma!" he bellowed. Nearby a cormorant grunted in protest, the only noise besides Emma's rapid footfalls.

Ignoring the cold on his bare feet and torso, he started after her, calling her name yet again. She didn't stop. In fact, when he hollered, she picked up her pace, going from a brisk walk to a jog to finally an all-out run. He followed her as far as the sidewalk, in time to see her jump into her car and peel off.

What the hell? Confusion swirled in his muzzy brain. It didn't make sense. They had a good time together. Check that, they had an *amazing* time together. Making love was a near religious experience, at least for him. No, for both of them. She was enjoying their time together as much as he was. So why cut and run when they still had several days left to enjoy each others' company?

"Hey, be grateful," he said to himself. "She's right, you don't do relationships." He'd been dreading saying goodbye, anyway. That was half the reason he'd invited her to Saint Martin, right? To postpone the unpleasantness. Now he didn't have to feel bad. Emma had done him a favor. He should be relieved. He could move on with a clean conscience.

Slowly, he walked back to the boat, waiting for the relief to wash over him.

It didn't come.

A week later, Gideon stomped into his cabin, feeling cold and miserable. Hinckley opened an irritated eye as he barged past on his way to the galley and the coffeepot. Which, he soon discovered, had about an inch of coffee left in it.

"Damn!" He slammed the pot on the burner, sending a metallic rattle reverberating through the boat. He was going to have to make a fresh pot, and the blasted canister was empty. What idiot had decided living on the water was a good idea, anyway? His hands were so numb he could barely feel them. How hadn't he noticed how cold Boston Harbor was before?

Blowing on his fingers, trying to jump-start some kind of circulation, he scanned the supplies, looking for a spare can of coffee. If he had to make instant, he would not be responsible for the damage. As he reviewed the various cans, his eyes fell on a bright red box. A sinking sensation hit him in the gut. Tea. Emma's tea.

He leaned a shoulder against the wall. It had been seven days since she'd pronounced them over and had taken off. Seven long days. He'd tried to reach her. She conveniently managed to be absent whenever he arrived at the Fairlane, and she wouldn't take his calls. He'd left messages at work, on her cell phone. In fact, he'd left so many messages he was starting to feel like a stalker.

This desperation wasn't like him. He didn't chase women. But Emma… He couldn't get her out of his head. No woman had ever gotten under his skin the way she had. He thought about her when he ate, when he showered, when he worked on the boat. The worst was at night, when he lay alone in his bed with nothing but thoughts of Emma to lie with him.

The simple truth was he missed her. Missed making her smile. Missed hearing her gentle breathing as she slept. Missed the fullness that swelled in his chest when she looked in his direction.

Conversely, the past week had brought him closer to his family than he'd been in years. Since their awkward conversation the other day, he and his father had forged some new bonds. Tentative ones, but he had hope they would grow strong. For the first time in his life, both of them were talking—really talking—and more importantly, listening. They discovered they shared a lot of traits, such as pride and stubbornness, and Gideon was starting to wonder if maybe DNA didn't matter, after all. He was even reconsidering Mariah's offer to take over Kent Hotels.

A decision he'd love to discuss with Emma.

His back pocket buzzed, telling him he had a call. The Fairlane, according to the call screen. When he saw the number, his pulse quickened. Maybe his stalking had finally paid off.

It hadn't. Mariah's voice greeted him from the other end. "Good morning to you, too," she said.

"Sorry, Grandmother." He tried to push the disappointment from his voice. "I was hop— I thought you were someone else."

"I'll forgive you, since you called me Grandmother."

He smiled to himself. "What can I do for you, *Grandmother?*"

"You can come to tea," she replied. "I want you to look at some concepts the advertising agency sent over."

"Isn't that Andrew's concern?"

"I want you to see them."

Gideon shook his head. He wondered if, in his grandmother's mind, he'd ever turned down her offer. "All right," he replied, "I'll be there. What time?"

"One o'clock."

"Sounds good. I'll see you then." Emma, too, he realized with a thrill. That is, if she didn't hide again.

Suddenly, an idea hit him. "Grandmother," he said, "will you do me a favor?"

"Make sure those letters go out in today's mail," Mrs. Kent said. "Tell Marketing and Legal I don't want them bickering about the words, either."

"Yes, ma'am," Emma answered, not entirely certain what she was answering "yes" to. Since breaking things off with Gideon, she'd been on autopilot. Her perpetual fog showed, too. She made stupid mistakes. Yesterday, she'd even sent a phone call through to Mrs. Kent during *All My Loves*.

Speaking of Mrs. Kent, her boss's pale blue eyes were impossibly intent as they studied Emma. "Is your headache any better today?" she asked in concern.

"A little," Emma replied. A migraine was the excuse she'd given for yesterday's mistake. It wasn't too much of a lie. She did have a headache.

"Hmmm, maybe you should see someone." Mrs. Kent was frowning now.

"I'll be fine." There was only one person she wanted to see, and he was off-limits. "I should be feeling better soon."

After all, it had been seven days, for crying out loud. Her mother bounced back in two. Emma should be over Gideon by now. Instead, he dominated her every thought. Every time she heard him on her voice mail, it was like a knife in her midsection. She was beginning to wonder if she'd ever stop thinking of him.

Mrs. Kent had a few more housekeeping items for review, so Emma forced herself back to the present as best she could. Still, she only half listened. Hopefully, her automatic notes would fill in the blanks. When her meeting was over she walked robotically back to her desk. If she was lucky, work would distract her for a few hours at least.

"Hello, Emma."

She stumbled, she stopped so quickly. Gideon stood in the doorway. Every emotion she'd been struggling to forget rushed at her simultaneously, forcing her to grab hold of the printer table for balance.

"I didn't know you were stopping by." He looked more handsome than a week ago. Obviously, he hadn't spent the past week tossing and turning the night away.

She didn't want to think how he did spend the night, either.

"I asked Mariah not to say anything. So you wouldn't have a chance to hide," he added when she frowned.

"I haven't been hiding," Emma snapped. She hated that he'd read her thoughts. "I've been very busy. Your grandmother is making up for the work she missed while in the hospital."

"Then why haven't you returned my calls?"

"I just told you. I've been very busy."

"Liar." Challenge sparkled in his eyes. Emma looked away. She didn't have the energy to fake an argument, so she surrendered. "I didn't see the need," she said, fiddling with the table edge. "We said everything that needed to be said the other night."

"Really? As I recall, you did all the talking."

"You didn't argue."

"You didn't give me a chance. You blindsided me, then took off before I could recover."

"I didn't think we had anything more to say."

His voice dropped a notch. "I've missed you, Emma. You're a hard woman to let go."

He spoke plainly, without a shred of seduction. The simplicity was far more devastating, anyway. "If I'd reacted faster the other night, I never would have let you walk off the boat. I would have taken you out to sea and refused to let you go."

In spite of herself, Emma had to smile at the image. "Pretty big gesture for a guy who doesn't believe in relationships," she said.

"Guess I'm not ready for this relationship to end yet."

"*Yet.* That's the magic word, isn't it?"

"What are you talking about?"

"You said yet." She leaned against the table. "You miss me now and you don't want our affair to end yet." Meaning eventually it would still end.

"What should I have said?"

How about, *Don't go. I love you.*

Suddenly, in one fell swoop, it hit her. She'd become her mother. Despite all her safeguards, all her vows of maintaining perspective, she'd fallen, anyway. Emma was in love with Gideon. She didn't want *yet.* She wanted *more.* She wanted him to love her back.

An impossible desire, to say the least.

"That's what happens when you look beyond a comfortable bed," she muttered.

"What?" Gideon seemed completely baffled.

"Nothing. You wouldn't understand."

"Try me."

She didn't want to. Now that her feelings had made their way to the surface, she needed to leave. To put some distance between them before she made a fool of herself.

Check that, a bigger fool. She pushed herself toward her desk. "I have to go meet with Marketing. Your grandmother wants this letter to go out today and Legal has a problem with some of the language. I need to—"

"Don't dodge my questions. You said something about a comfortable bed. What was it?" He paused, and she saw understanding crest in his eyes. "Does this have something to do with what you said the other night? About nursing fantasies?"

Trust him to listen too well. "Let it go, Gideon. What I said or didn't say doesn't matter."

"It does to me." His fingers wrapped around her forearm. "I'm not letting you go until you tell me what you meant."

"Your grandmother—"

"When will you learn that my grandmother can wait?"

Emma looked down at the hand on her arm, gentle but immovable. "Fine," she snapped. Maybe if she explained, he'd understand and finally leave her alone. "I said this is what happens when you look for more than a comfortable bed. You end up wanting too much."

"Too much?"

"As in things you can't have."

His eyes were two probing blue beams. "What is it you want, Emma?"

"What do you think I want?" she retorted, furiously yanking free of his grasp. A week's worth of fatigue and misery finally got the best of her, and all her frustration and pain just bubbled over. "The happy ending, the fairy tale. I want you not to say 'yet.' I want you!"

She slapped her hand to her mouth. Oh Lord, she hadn't meant to say that.

Gideon stepped back, stunned. Her cheeks felt on fire. Maybe they were. Could she be a bigger idiot? Why not scream "I love you" too, and make her humiliation complete? Hot angry tears sprang to her eyes as she groped desperately on her desk for something, anything, she could use as an excuse to escape this hideous embarrassment. She settled for a random stack of papers. "I have to go to talk to Marketing…."

"Wait."

"No. I've already said too much. Let me go." She tore herself away from his restraining hand and practically ran out of the office.

She wanted him, thought Gideon, dazed. His chest was so full he swore it would burst. It was as if a missing piece of him slid into place. Emma wanted him….

"Are you going to stand there daydreaming, or are you going to chase her down?"

He turned around to see Mariah in the doorway. How long had she been listening? She admonished him with a sharp stare. "Well?" she asked imperiously.

Her question kickstarted him into action. "Excuse me, Grandmother." He left the room at a run. This time Emma wasn't going to make a proclamation and then walk away. Not without hearing him out.

*She wanted him.* And she was standing by the elevator, trying to escape.

"Don't you dare leave this floor, Emma O'Rourke!" He bellowed so loudly a nearby housekeeper dropped her towels. Emma, though, true to form, didn't pause a beat. In fact, she pushed the elevator button.

"Son of a—" He jogged down the hallway toward her. "You are not running away from me before I can say my piece, do you hear me?"

She jabbed at the button again. "What else is there to say, Gideon? I wanted something you can't give. You said so yourself."

"So you simply walk away?"

"It's called cutting my losses," she said shortly.

Cutting her… For crying out loud. Frustration ripped through him. "Dammit Emma, how am I supposed to get through to you."

The elevator doors opened. Emma stepped on, but he threw his arm between the doors, preventing them from closing.

"I thought you were kidding about that bed. I can't believe you actually think that way."

"Well, where I come from, there's no sense wanting more than you can have," she retorted hotly.

"Instead you decide to want nothing at all?"

Emma glared at him indignantly. "What's that suppose to mean?"

"It means you're afraid."

"I am not afraid," she almost snarled, stepping off the elevator.

"Aren't you? You said it yourself. You're afraid you'll like life so much you'll want more. So you abstain altogether. No harm, no foul, right?"

Emma's temper finally snapped, because he was so utterly right. "Can you blame me? Do you have any idea what it's like watching your mother fall for man after man on some fruitless search for the one of her dreams? Do you know how many times I had my life tossed upside down because she was certain this week's Prince Charming was 'the one'? I promised myself I would never be disappointed the way she was. That I wasn't going to spend the rest of my life regretting or mourning something I could never have."

Gideon looked at the ground. Emma's furious confession had knocked him square in the gut. "I don't know what to say."

"There's nothing to say," she stated coldly,

reining in her anger. "I said all along I knew what I was getting into. You don't have to feel guilty."

Guilty? Her words sent a fresh round of frustration rolling through him, and he groaned aloud. "Will you stop?"

"What? All I said was that I knew what I was—"

"I know what you were saying. Would you stop assuming I don't want a commitment?" God, he wanted to throttle her then and there.

She was looking up at him, wide-eyed with disbelief, waiting for his next comment. A thousand tangled emotions stormed in her beautiful brown eyes. *Amazing,* Gideon thought suddenly. He could look at those eyes forever and never figure out every different emotion.

*Forever.*

The word hit him like a stone. His whole life, he'd mocked the idea, but when it came to Emma, the word *forever* flowed effortlessly. The fight went out of him, and when he spoke again, his voice was calm.

"How would you know what I want,

Emma?" he asked. "You've never let me participate in the conversation."

"Of course I did. You never answered."

"Because you always ran away. The other night. This afternoon. Even the first night we made love you had me out the door before I could catch my breath. You've never given me a chance to say anything."

Emma blinked in shock. She'd given him plenty of chances.

Hadn't she?

But that didn't matter. The fact remained he wasn't going to hang around. "I heard you tell your father you didn't plan to stay."

"My father? When did I say…?" He paused as comprehension dawned. "Now I remember. Last week, after breakfast. You were eavesdropping."

"I was coming around the corner when I heard you," she said defensively. "You told your father you had no reason to stay in Boston."

"I was talking family. Not about you."

"Great," she said with a bitter laugh, "I didn't even make the equation. I feel so much better now."

She turned to summon the elevator again,

only to have Gideon lift her arm away before she could push the button. "What I meant," he said, "was that I was planning to take you with me. Remember? That's why there was nothing keeping me here.

"Look," he continued, "I know what it's like to have your parents' love lives turn your own life upside down. Believe me, I know that chaos better than you think. And until recently—very recently—I followed the low-expectations road, too. Stay away from relationships, stay out of trouble. But I'm realizing that road might not be the safest one, after all."

"Why not?"

Cupping her cheek, he forced her eyes to meet his. "Because I met a Little Match Girl, and I didn't realize how cold and lonely my boat would be without her on board."

Emma stared into his blue eyes, looking for some sign, any sign, that she shouldn't believe him. Of course, it was hard to tell with her own eyes tearing the way they were. "Your boat's cold?"

"Freezing. Quiet, too. Don't tell him I said so, but Hinckley's a lousy berth mate.

He just doesn't spoon into my body the way you do."

Emma looked away. "So you're looking for a bed warmer."

"I'm looking for a first mate," Gideon replied, drawing her attention back. "I told you before, you'd make a terrific one. The job's yours if you're interested."

"First mate, huh?"

Gideon nodded and she smiled shyly. She'd never heard such a wonderful offer.

But… She caught herself before she could accept. What if she was reading too much into the invitation? What if she was making the same mistake again?

*Protect yourself,* a voice urged. All the old familiar voices chimed in. *Be realistic. Don't get your hopes up. You'll only get your heart broken.* She saw her mother crying pitifully over yet another failed relationship. Did Emma want to end up like that?

But wasn't she already miserable? Wasn't being with Gideon even for a short while better than the heartache she was enduring now? Longing rose up inside her, urging her to take a chance.

"I'm scared."

She didn't realize she'd spoken aloud until Gideon smiled and brushed his thumb across her cheek. "Me, too. Thinking long-term is uncharted water for me."

"Same here," Emma replied.

"Then I guess we'll have to navigate those waters together."

*Together.* The word held such hope and promise. With tears of happiness filling her eyes, Emma smiled and buried her face in the crook of his neck. Gideon wrapped his arms around her tightly. "I've missed you so much," he whispered as he kissed her temple.

"I've missed *you*," she told him in a choked voice.

They stood quietly, letting the warmth and safety of being in each other's arms wash over them. After a few moments—or an hour, Emma wasn't sure—Gideon pulled back, revealing eyes that were bluer and brighter than anything she'd ever seen. The emotion shining in their depths was unmistakable, and her heart swelled with love. "So," he said with a smile, "are you up for the voyage, Miss O'Rourke?"

She caressed his jaw. "For as long as it takes, Mr. Kent."

"Good. Because I have a feeling it's going to be a very long journey."

"How long?"

He moved closer, bringing his breath to her lips. "How do you feel about forever?"

Emma didn't think it was possible, but her heart filled even more. "Forever sounds perfect, Captain." She leaned forward to complete the kiss.

Suddenly a thought came to her, and she pulled back. "Your grandmother," she gasped. "She's probably wondering what happened. We should go explain."

"Oh, we've got time," Gideon replied. With a triumphant smile, he showed her the time on his wristwatch. "It's two o'clock."

Three months later, Emma stood on deck, watching the sun fall off the edge of the earth in all its breathtaking glory.

"Beautiful," she murmured.

A pair of strong arms wrapped her waist from behind. "So, is it everything I promised?" Gideon asked, pulling her to him. She leaned into his chest, marveling for the millionth time how safe and happy his embrace made her.

"More than everything," she said.

"Good. After all, we aim to please." He nipped the curve of her neck. "And please, and please, and please…"

Nipping became nuzzling, and Emma giggled. She'd had no idea life could be this magical.

Gideon had made peace once and for all with his family. He told her about his parentage; how his mother didn't know who had fathered her son. Emma agreed with Mariah and the others. His DNA didn't matter. He was a Kent at heart. It took a while, but Gideon was slowly realizing that same fact.

At the moment, however, he appeared more interested in peppering her shoulders with kisses. The man was insatiable. Not that Emma minded. Making love to Gideon never grew old. They discovered something new about each other every time.

"Mmm," she said, letting her head fall back to allow him better access. "I'm going to hate going back to work, after all this sunshine."

"Well, we can always extend the honeymoon another few weeks." He teased her ear with his tongue. "Or years."

"Don't you have a hotel chain to run?" Last

night, he'd called his grandmother to officially agree to be her successor. They were scheduled to meet with the board of directors next week.

"I suppose," he replied with a sigh. He didn't bother disguising his disappointment. "Though running a hotel chain isn't nearly as fun as teaching you how to sail."

"Oh, is that what we're calling it now," she teased. "If it helps, I'll be right by your side." She planted a kiss on his nose. "Just like a good first mate should."

"You, sweetheart, are hardly a first mate. More like a co-captain."

"How about admiral?"

"As long as we've got Hinckley, I'm afraid that position is filled." With that, Gideon adjusted their positions so his mouth hovered just above hers. "Have I told you today how much I love you, Mrs. Kent?"

Emma smiled. "Yes, but I'll never get tired of hearing it. Or telling you I love you back."

And as the sun disappeared, she kissed him with all the happiness she felt in her heart.

"Thank you," she whispered, "for giving me everything."

Everything, she thought to herself, and more.

# LARGER-PRINT BOOKS!
## GET 2 FREE LARGER-PRINT NOVELS PLUS
## 2 FREE GIFTS!

HARLEQUIN® *Romance*

### From the Heart, For the Heart

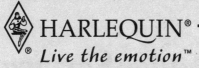